CELEBRITIES, AUTHORS, AND EXPERTS APPLAUD . . .

KIDS CAN SAVE THE ANIMALS!

"It's positively *scary* how some people treat animals! KIDS CAN SAVE THE ANIMALS! gives you 101 *frighteningly* good ideas on how you can make a difference!"

—Elvira, Mistress of the Dark

• • •

"Compassion: Kids may not know how to spell it, but they sure know what it means. This book shows them how to *live* it."

—Berke Breathed, author of
Bloom County and *Outland* comic strips

• • •

"Full of great ideas for turning positive feeling for animals into practical action that will keep animal liberation moving forward into the next generations."

—Peter Singer, author of *Animal Liberation*

(*continued*)

"This delightful straightforward book not only helps children recognize animal abuse, but gives them constructive things they can do about it! Harnessing all that youthful energy is a great idea. Buy this book for your children and READ IT YOURSELF!"

    —Rue McClanahan, co-star of "The Golden Girls"

. . .

"This wonderful book empowers children with information and a way they themselves can make a difference."

    —Sally Struthers, actress
    and children's rights activist

. . .

"Full of fun. . . . The entire La Russa family enjoyed it—it gave us a lot of ways to help animals."

    —Tony La Russa, manager of the Oakland A's

. . .

"If you would like to make our world a nicer place, this book is a great way to start."

    —Jane Wiedlin, musician

. . .

"Every generation leaves its historic mark. Using the practical wisdom in this book, the next generation—today's children—will be known as the generation that saved the animals."

    —Tom Regan, author of *The Case for Animal Rights*
    and president of the Culture and Animals Foundation

"If you are a kid who wants to bring a little more love into the world, this book is for you. If you read it, you will be filled with ideas that you can do to help make the lives of animals happier."

> —**John Robbins,** author of *Diet for a New America*
> and president of EarthSave;
> and **Ocean Robbins,** co-founder of the YES! Tour
> (Youth for Environmental Sanity)

• • •

"Full of terrific ideas . . . with educational, inspirational, and amusing activities that can help children grow up with a healthy regard for animals and the earth."

> —**Kim Bartlett,** editor of
> *The Animals' Agenda* magazine

• • •

"A masterpiece without equal. . . . Factual and practical, yet gentle and considerate. Never before has the art of teaching children compassion for all life been so thoughtfully written. A must for parents, teachers and children alike."

> —**Laura Moretti,** editor-in-chief of
> *The Animals' Voice Magazine*

• • •

"An empowering book that gives kids the information they need to help protect other Earthlings who share our home planet. I recommend it highly to anyone who believes that other animals have just as much right to live here as people do."

> —**Jackie Kaufman,** publisher of
> *P3: The Earth-Based Magazine for Kids*

• • • *(continued)*

"Contains many amazingly practical suggestions. It motivated me to become active and more aware. I am now starting a kids' animals rights newsletter. Thanks stacks for writing it."

—**Esther Singer,** 12 years old, daughter of Peter Singer, author of *Animal Liberation*

• • •

"I wish I had had a book like this when I was a kid. You can bet the kids who come to see me on tour will hear about it."

—**Mike Vallely,** professional skateboarder

• • •

"This upbeat, sensible book helps you make a huge difference, a little bit at a time. Don't grow up without it!"

—**Sabrina LeBeauf,** actress

KIDS CAN SAVE THE ANIMALS!

101 EASY THINGS TO DO

INGRID NEWKIRK

National Director, People for the Ethical Treatment of Animals (PETA)

WARNER BOOKS

A Time Warner Company

Warner Books, Inc., 666 Fifth Avenue, New York, NY 10103

A Time Warner Company

Printed in the United States of America
First printing: August 1991
10 9 8 7 6 5 4 3 2 1

Library of Congress Cataloging-in-Publication Data
Newkirk, Ingrid.
    Kids can save the animals! : 101 easy things to do / Ingrid
Newkirk.
        p.   cm.
    Summary: Discusses the many ways in which people can help animals,
ease their living conditions, and make sure they receive the proper
treatment which is their right.
    ISBN 0-446-39271-5
        1. Animal welfare—Juvenile literature.   2. Humane education—
Juvenile literature.   [1. Animals—Treatment.   2. Animal rights.]
    I. Title.
    HV4708.N494 1991
    179'.3—dc20   91-9550
                                                                      CIP
                                                                      AC

COVER DESIGN: *Anne Twomey*
COVER ILLUSTRATION: *Susan Hellard*
TEXT ILLUSTRATIONS: *Susan Hellard*
BOOK DESIGN: *Giorgetta Bell McRee*

... this is the time for thinking
Quite revisionary thoughts
About bats, dinosaurs and other creatures
Of weird and wonderful sorts.

—**ANN COTTRELL FREE**
No Room, Save in the Heart

This book is dedicated to all those
who have thought enough about animals
to do something for them.

CONTENTS

ACKNOWLEDGMENTS

When Warner gave the green light for this book, PETA was being sued by a Las Vegas showman named Bobby Berosini. We had received a videotape of Berosini punching and beating the orangutans he uses in his nightclub comedy act. PETA had condemned the actions publicly, and Berosini was trying to put us out of business. Our days were taken up defending the right to expose what those gentle ''people of the forest'' had endured to make people laugh.

Between court sessions, bits of this book and messages about it were being faxed between Nevada and Washington, D.C., where Kym Boyman, my special assistant, made soup from scribbles. For being ''book mother,'' which is a task not easily accomplished, the thanks go to Kym.

Children and other-than-human beings have great allies in the form of the PETA correspondents. Their hard work and good humor made this book possible. They are the wonderful and witty Karin Bennett and Teresa Gibbs, Christine Jackson (who should stick to writing eloquent prose—the joke she made up was one of the worst I've ever heard!), Carla Bennett (the ''Ask Carla'' columnist who really does know *every-*

thing), Jill Leonard, and Donna Marsden, a dog's best friend. Thanks also go to Nancy Valerga, who good-naturedly researched the answers to such odd questions as how many babies can a mother cockroach have!

For proofreading the manuscript and keeping us in line, we are grateful to Karen Porreca, and for typing the whole thing, Robyn Wesley.

Special thanks go to June Brody, Dorothy Darby, Adam May and Patty Shenker for their generous contributions.

Of all the organizations and individuals kind enough to give us materials and ideas, the Animal Welfare Institute, the Vegetarian Resource Group, Hope Buyukmihci of the Unexpected Wildlife Refuge, Candy Forest and Nancy Schimmel of Sisters' Choice, and Donna Smith of the Peninsula Humane Society deserve special mention.

And, of course, Joann Davis, Colleen Kaplin, and Warner have our thanks for helping PETA help kids help the animals!

SPECIAL NOTE TO PARENTS AND TEACHERS FROM THE AUTHOR

In this book you will find suggestions for all sorts of things children can do to help their natural friends, the animals. Older generations, including my own, were shortchanged; most of us loved animals with all our hearts, yet most of us dissected a frog, dreamed of wearing a fur coat, and were persuaded not to think where our meals came from. Today's generation *wants* not just to be honest about what happens to the animals, but to make a difference. These kids are destined to teach us some excellent lessons!

If you would like more detailed information on any topic in this book, please do not hesitate to write me personally at **PETA,** P.O. Box 42516, Washington, DC 20015.

FOREWORD

Our awareness of animal abuse has become "right up there" with our awareness of human injustice and environmental devastation. That's why I'm really glad to be a part of KIDS CAN SAVE THE ANIMALS! 101 EASY THINGS TO DO. It is the latest contribution to a sane and loving world and there isn't anything left out of it.

When I was seven years old, I became a vegan, meaning I stopped eating animals and using products that were created by hurting animals. Not only I, but my entire family. My sister Rain was five years old then, Leaf was three, Liberty was one, and Summer, my youngest sister, had just been born.

That was over thirteen years ago and, although we didn't know then all we know today—that animals are losing their habitat because forests are being cut down, that dolphins and whales are being destroyed and swim in polluted seas, and that conditions for animals on factory farms and in pounds can be terrible—we wanted to use our voices on behalf of voiceless animals.

Back then, it was a lonely decision. We knew of no other children who felt the way we did or books to help us feel part of a caring movement. Today, our lifestyle is much, much easier! The good news is that lots of children care and want to get involved to save the planet and all the different life forms who call Earth their home.

> We are all a part of the earth
> And it is part of us.
> The perfumed flowers are our sisters;
> The deer, the horse, the great eagle,
> These are our brothers.
>
> All things are connected,
> Like the blood which unites one family.
> All things are connected.
>
> —Words of Chief Seattle

I hope that this book will be a friend to you and give you strength.
—RIVER PHOENIX

INTRODUCTION

When I was a young person about your age (and that was more years ago than I care to tell you!) I had a favorite aunt. Her name was Aunt Lucy, and she was regarded by many people in our small New England town as being a rather peculiar old lady, because she rescued stray dogs and cats. Aunt Lucy had a very big house, with lots of lawns and gardens around it, but instead of spending her money on her house, or herself, she spent it on the creatures she saved. And a few of the animals she couldn't find homes for always lived with her.

I did not regard Aunt Lu as being peculiar in any way. Rather I loved her very much, and I thought she had the most interesting life of any grownup that I knew. I loved to go to her house after school and have several whole hours of what she called "stray play." And it was on a day that I was playing with some of Aunt Lu's rescued friends that I resolved always to be a friend to animals myself, and to help them in any way I could when I got bigger.

The problem was—how to be a *good* friend? Animals are fragile creatures, and you need all the information you can get on the best ways to help them, and to save them from trouble. What I was searching for was a book with such information, but back in those days, such a book did not exist.

Today, I am happy to say, such a book *does* exist—and this is it. Written by one of the top experts in the country, this book will introduce you to the wonderful world of saving animals. You will learn of hundreds of exciting groups that can provide you with intriguing projects about specific animal problems. You will learn about animals all around the world, and probably learn something you didn't know about your own companion animal right at home—and how to make his or her life happier and longer. And, most important of all, you will learn of simple habits you can form which, if you make them strong habits and stick to them as you grow older, will do more to help your animal friends than anything else you can think of.

This book can turn you into a real "animal person." But that doesn't mean it's a hard book to read. Rather it is a wonderful book to read because the author has a terrific sense of humor, and because saving animals is a terrific thing to do. Indeed, I believe that saving animals is one of the most enjoyable and satisfying things you will *ever* do, even if you live to be as old as me!

—CLEVELAND AMORY

PREFACE

When I was about eight years old, I left the little English town of Ware ("Where?" my new friends would ask), left my school and everyone I knew, and headed off, with my parents, to a very different life *thousands* of miles away in India.

From that moment on everything was different. The ocean liner we took on our two-week voyage was many stories tall, and when I first started walking up the gangplank, I felt so frightened that my knees wobbled. It didn't seem possible that such a huge, heavy skyscraper of a ship could float! That first night, everyone became ill from the motion of the waves, and I wished I could go home again.

Out in the open ocean there were animals I had never seen before: flying fishes, giant turtles, and manta rays. Dolphins leaped out of the water, chasing the ship's bow. At night there was only the light of the moon, no land or other ships to be seen. During the day there was only water, stretching from horizon to horizon.

When we arrived in Bombay, big birds called "kites" circled in the sky. There were even vultures and parrots to watch. Camels, bullocks, and men pulled carts through the streets. Everything we ate was odd:

fruits called lichees and guavas, figure-eight candies called *gulabjamins,* spicy curries, and little pastries cut into triangles and fried in vats of oil on the street.

Some people spoke English, but most spoke one of the many Indian languages. It was peculiar to hear everyone chatting but not have any idea what they were saying. When I spoke, Indian children would giggle at me. On the train, my father began to teach me to count—*ek, do, tin, char*—and how to say "please" and "thank you" in Hindustani.

Sometimes I think my experience must be a little bit like what animals go through in today's world. We don't speak their language, and perhaps we laugh at them sometimes when they are trying to tell us something serious.

Our clothes, our cars, our foods, the things we do that seem ordinary to us, must be very strange to them. Other-than-human beings look terrific in the feathers, fur, and hair they were born with! In their own homelands, they eat well and stay healthy on natural foods, like nuts, berries, seeds, fruits, and vegetables. To keep happy, they play chase, sing, sunbathe, and invent simple games. Can you imagine a dog buying a party dress, a cow ordering out for pizza, or a bat playing a video game?

Sometimes, animals from faraway countries are forced to leave their friends behind, just as I had to. I was very lucky because my parents came with me. Whenever I was frightened, they explained what was happening and that everything would be all right. My trip was comfortable, too. No such luck for the animals. Those captured in South America for a New York pet shop or torn from their mothers' arms in Africa for an American zoo can be crammed into a small cage in the hold of a ship or smuggled—even upside down—in the false linings of suitcases. Many die on their voyages, and those who survive find a life that is often lonely and very sad. No one speaks their language, and they are often ignored or misunderstood.

When you think about it, what many animals go through is pretty awful, but there's no point in being glum when we can easily make things better. There are *tons* of things we can do to help animals and to make sure they *do* enjoy life: things we can make and buy, things we can say, ways we can stick up for the animals just by knowing their likes and dislikes and by making sure other people get to know them, too.

Alex Pacheco and I formed People for the Ethical Treatment of

Animals in 1980 to let people know what animals go through in our world and to encourage everyone to pitch in to make the animals' plight better. Today there are over 350,000 PETA kids and adult PETA members speaking up for other-than-human beings. That's pretty exciting!

As you read this book, you will probably think of lots of other ideas that aren't in here because there are as many ways to help animals as there are kids in the world. I'd love to hear *your* ideas, so please write to me at PETA to let me know what *you* are doing to save the animals. *Good luck!*

1 DO UNTO OTHERS...

To understand any living being you must creep within and feel the beating of his heart.

— **W. Macneile Dixon**

Animals have feelings, just as you and I do. Just like us, they feel the heat and cold, the sun and rain. Just like us, they enjoy a comfortable place to live, good food, and loving attention. They miss you when you are away, and they remember things that have happened to them.

DID YOU KNOW?

- When Princess Beatrix of Holland was a child, she forgot one day to feed her dog. The next morning she was served no breakfast, on the orders of her father, Prince Bernhard. (What lesson do you think she learned?)
- The phrase *in the doghouse* means "in disgrace." This says a lot about how little people can care about their dog's living space.

1

- Most other-than-human beings have better-developed senses than people. A bloodhound's sense of smell is roughly two million times as sensitive as ours, so paint, cigarette smoke, air "fresheners," and cooking smells can really get to them.
- Domestic birds, rodents, and rabbits like to fly, splash in water, burrow, hop, and do all the fun and fulfilling things their free-roaming relatives do.

WHAT YOU CAN DO

Cats and Dogs

- Think how you would feel in your animal friends' place. Give yourself a point for anything in this section you do right. Then total up the points at the end and see how you rate. As a cat and/ or dog guardian, do you:

  - give them clean, fresh water in a clean bowl?
  - let them sleep inside with you or in a safe, snug shelter? They should have a soft, dry bed to keep them off the drafty floors and should never sleep outside in the cold!
  - give them a variety of food they enjoy and that's healthy for them?
  - allow them plenty of playtime with you and other household and neighborhood companions?
  - give them plenty of chances to relieve themselves (at least four to five times each day)? Is their litter box/yard always clean?
  - teach them rules with patience and kindness? They should never be hit or scolded. Humane societies have dog training and cat care booklets you can use.
  - feed them *before* you sit down to eat? When they're finished, do you say, "All gone," and make an "empty hands" signal with upturned palms, followed by a pat, so they won't expect food while you're eating?
  - make sure their collar is sized correctly? (Three fingers should fit under it.) Do you check it often, especially if your companion is still growing?

• groom your friends every day if they need it? They should get brushed and combed and their coat checked for fleas and ticks. Powdered brewer's yeast and garlic in their food can free them from harsh flea powders, sprays, and collars. A flea comb catches fleas in its teeth, so your companions won't have to use theirs.
• give signs that your friends are loved, like a friendly word, a scratch behind their ears, and treats?

● How did you score? Nine to ten points means you're a pretty perfect guardian. Five to eight points means there's work to be done. Four points or fewer means there's an animal emergency in your house.

Birds

● Birds normally live in flocks; they love companionship and space to fly. A lone bird in a cage is a sad sight. Parrots may pluck out their own feathers if they are unhappy or stressed; some birds will rock back and forth endlessly. How do you rate as a bird guardian? Do birds in your care have:

• at least one bird companion?
• enough cage room to fly in, such as part or all of a room?
• windows (to see out of—not go out of)?
• lots of perches?
• a seed dish always full of food (not hulls—the outer casing—which they spit back into their dishes)?
• something to sharpen their beaks on, such as a heavy, nonsplintering piece of wood?
• fresh fruits, vegetables, and water?
• gravel (to digest their food)?
• water to splash and bathe in, as well as to drink?
• toys (parakeets love measuring spoons)?

Rodents

- Do gerbils, guinea pigs, hamsters, rats, and mice have:

  - a space they can call their own, like upside-down boxes with holes cut in them?
  - a comfortable cage? (A metal tray floor covered with newspaper sheets makes the best floor—wire mesh is quite painful to stand and walk on, and wood is hard to clean.)
  - a cage large enough so they can scamper around? (Store-bought cages are tiny—write to **PETA** to learn how to make a more suitable cage.)
  - things to climb and play in, like paper towel rolls, shelves, and old socks?
  - an exercise wheel?
  - things to chew on, like tree branches or other hard, chemical-free wood, to keep their teeth worn down?
  - raisins and other food treats hidden in the cage?

- Rodents' cages should be cleaned *at least* once a week (more often if necessary), and your small friends will love some supervised time outside of their cage every day.
- Here's a tip: If you have both males and females, keep them in separate cages so you don't end up with a tribe of small animals. Female rodents can live nicely together, except for hamsters, who prefer to be alone. Most male rodents will fight with each other.

Rabbits

- If you have rabbits who are kept outside, check that their hutch is totally dogproof and weatherproof and is raised on legs at least two feet off the ground. Does the hutch have:

  - a large screened outdoor area for stretching out and fresh air?
  - a snug nest box of solid plywood?
  - lots of hay for burrowing?
  - roofing shingles attached on the outside of the box to protect it from bad weather?

• Here's a tip: Avoid bringing rabbits in and out of the house if the air-conditioning and heat are on during weather extremes, since rabbits are very sensitive to dampness and changes in temperature. Be sure to switch the hutch from outdoors to indoors before cold weather comes.

• If you have small caged animals, put a star by the things in this chapter you'd like to start doing to improve their lives.

CHECK IT OUT

• Make a list of everything you can do to make life consistently great for each animal in your household. Tape the list where you can check it every day. This way, you won't forget they're depending on you!

• If you have hamsters, other rodents, birds, or rabbits, write to **PETA,** P.O. Box 42516, Washington, DC 20015, for more free tips on how to brighten their lives.

2 RESCUE THE RAIN FORESTS!

If the beasts were gone, men would die from a great loneliness of spirit. For whatever happens to the beasts, soon happens to man. All things are connected.

—CHIEF SEATTLE, 1854

DID YOU KNOW?

- It is always warm and muggy in the rain forests, like a steamy bathroom after a hot shower. The moisture and warmth allows the trees to keep their leaves all year long and so provide food for many animals who live there. Hercules beetles as big as baseballs roam the forest, colorful parrots called "scarlet macaws" fly from tree to tree with wings that measure three feet from tip to tip, and howler monkeys sound as if they're singing to each other across the forest when they warn of danger and defend their homes.
- Rain forests cover less than 2 percent of the entire planet's surface,

yet they are home to nearly half of all the plants and animals on earth!

- The rain forests run along the equator, the halfway mark between the North and South Poles. The largest rain forests are in South America, Southeast Asia, and West Africa, but Hawaii and Puerto Rico have important rain forests, too.
- The Rainforest Action Network estimates that four to fifteen species each day become extinct in the world's rain forests. The destruction of the rain forests is endangering the very existence of more than half of all the world's plant and animal species! Every year an area the size of the state of Pennsylvania is leveled in the tropical rain forests (that's equal to a football field every second)! Half of the world's rain forests are already gone.
- Human beings live in the rain forests, too. Their homes are being destroyed because, like the other-than-human beings, they are pretty powerless to fight back. Until recently, people made fun of the human forest dwellers, just as they make fun of the animals.
- In addition to being home to *billions* of animal species and lots of people, the trees in the rain forests make a lot of the oxygen we need to breathe right here in America. Without the forests, people could become extinct, too!

WHAT YOU CAN DO

- Ask your family to avoid buying and eating hamburgers. Most of the South American rain forests being chopped down (about 90 percent) are destroyed to provide ranchers with cheap grazing land for their cattle. For just one hamburger, fifty-five square feet of forest must be chopped down. Some fast-food restaurants tell us that they only buy beef stamped "U.S.," but that's a silly claim because all rain forest beef gets this stamp when it comes into the United States.
- Ask your family not to buy things made out of wood that comes from the rain forest, such as mahogany, teak, rosewood, and zebrawood. When your family is buying wood products, like furniture, ask the store salespeople lots of questions about what kind of wood you are buying and where it came from. If they can't

promise that the wood did *not* come from the rain forests, shop somewhere else. Better yet, always try to buy secondhand wood items from thrift shops, yard sales, or the "For Sale" section of the newspaper. Buying used items saves all kinds of trees, which are homes to all kinds of animals!

- Make a free call to the **Weyerhaeuser Company,** which is one of the largest importers of tropical rain forest wood, and ask them to stop buying trees chopped down in the rain forests. Their toll-free number is 1-800-525-5440. (Weyerhaeuser sells paper products and carries over two hundred brand names of disposable diapers. Boycott them all!)
- Make a free call to **Georgia-Pacific Products** for the same reason. Their toll-free number is 1-800-447-2882. Tell them their paper products won't be welcome at your house. Georgia-Pacific products include

  - **tissue paper:** Angel Soft, Cormatic, Mr. Big
  - **paper towels:** Sparkle, Delta, Mr. Big Paper
  - **paper napkins:** Coronet, Hudson, Soft Ply

- Use scrap paper, not fresh paper, for notes to friends and for doodling.

CHECK IT OUT

- Write to **The Children's Rainforest,** Box 936, Lewiston, MA 04240, to find out how you can help this group purchase land in the rain forests to be saved for the animals who need the forests to survive.
- Write to the **Rainforest Action Network,** 301 Broadway, Suite A, San Francisco, CA 94133, for more information about the rain forests and why we must save them.

3 LIBRARY LEARNING

A snake slithered into the local library and politely asked the lady behind the desk where he could find books on skin shedding and sunbathing.

"Well," said the lady, looking down at him over her glasses, "we don't carry books like that, and anyway, we don't serve snakes in here!"

"No wonder," said the snake, "with such a limited selection."

DID YOU KNOW?

- A library display can get hundreds of people to think about a subject.
- Most libraries leave a display up for a month.
- Most librarians welcome ideas for new displays.
- Most librarians like animals.
- Many people will read books they see in a library display.
- Many people don't even know there are any books about animal rights.

9

WHAT YOU CAN DO

- Make a great display. First, ask your school or local librarian to write to PETA on school or library writing paper for a free "Library Pack." Librarians can also receive free books, fact sheets, leaflets, and newsletters. Write to **PETA,** P.O. Box 42516, Washington, DC 20015.

  - The library pack is full of information sheets about animal rights for the library's files.
  - It also has coupons for many free books and videos and a colorful stand-up "Library Display Board."

- When the materials arrive, you and the librarian can make a display. Use the display board and lay the books out or stand them up around it. Leaflets about animal rights, and a leaflet holder, come with the display board. Put the leaflets where people can take them.
- When the display is taken down, give the display board to your local humane society or some other group who could use it, unless the librarian wants to keep it for next year.
- See what books, magazines, films, and videos about animals your library carries. If it doesn't have the ones listed in this book, ask your library staff to order them and give them the information to make it easier.

CHECK IT OUT

- When your school librarian sends for a PETA Library Pack, your school library will automatically be put on a list to receive future issues of *PETA News.* Ask him or her to request *PETA Kids* and *Brainstorm,* too.
- Send the New England Anti-Vivisection Society (NEAVS) the address of your school and the name of your school librarian, so that she or he will receive free mailings about animal rights. Write to **NEAVS,** 333 Washington St., Suite 850, Boston, MA 02108.

- Ask your librarian to send for the monthly publications *Kind News Jr.* (for grades two through four) and *Kind News Sr.* (for grades five and six) from the **National Association for Humane & Environmental Education (NAHEE)**, 67 Salem Rd., East Haddam, CT 06423.

• One copy is free to anyone who sends a stamped, self-addressed envelope with a written request.
• Subscriptions are available only in bundles of thirty-two copies each (they're meant for school classrooms). Each subscription includes *Kind Teacher*, a teachers' magazine with reproducible posters, games, daily calendar announcements, and lesson plans coordinated with *Kind News*. The September issue comes with Kind ID cards for students.

- More kids' animal protection magazines (see appendix B for addresses):

> *Animal Aid Youth Group Newsletter*
> *The Beaver Defenders*
> *The Dolphin Log*
> *Greenscene*
> *Otterwise*
> *OUT*
> *PETA Kids*
> *Trumpet*
> *Your Kindness Club Newsletter*

- For a list of books, including descriptions, see chapter 43. If your library doesn't have these, ask your librarian to order them. (And don't forget to ask for this book!)
- Encourage your library (and video store) to stock videos on animal issues such as *The Secret of NIMH, The Plague Dogs, The Little Mermaid, Animals Are Beautiful People,* and *Dr. Doolittle.* Some stores also loan public service videos, such as PETA's *Don't Kill the Animals* and *Exporting Cruelty.*
- Ask your librarian to contact **Focus on Animals,** P.O. Box 150, Trumbull, CT 06611, for a catalog of videotapes that promote

kindness toward animals. You must send $3 for the catalog, but the money will go toward the rental or purchase of the first film or video.

● Order a free "Student Pack" and/or "Teacher Pack" from PETA. Students receive twelve fact sheets, two magazines, and a handful of informative leaflets. Teachers receive the same, plus the book *Animal Liberation* and a booklet on alternatives to dissection.

4 DON'T PESTER THE PIGEONS

Pretty pigeons
On the ground and in the trees
When they're chased and yelled at
They get shaky knees.
        —**JESSICA HUBBARD,** age eight

Can you imagine sitting in the park, picnicking with friends, eating your sandwich, or trying to sleep, when all of a sudden people run right through your picnic and start chasing you? Sounds crazy, or at least extremely rude, doesn't it?

Well, many parents watch little kids do exactly those sorts of things to pigeons, starlings, and other birds who are resting peacefully on the grass or eating seeds or crumbs. Some parents don't give such behavior a second thought, and some kids think it's a hoot to watch the pigeons scurry away or have to abandon their activities—or their naps—to fly out of reach. It's easy to see that the birds aren't having any fun while this is going on. Their hearts are probably racing a mile a minute.

13

DID YOU KNOW?

- Starlings were brought to the United States in 1890 by a man who loved Shakespeare's plays. Since Shakespeare wrote about starlings in one of his plays, the traveler thought the United States wouldn't be complete without them.
- The pigeons we see in cities today are a kind of dove called a "rock dove." They were brought to the United States from Europe by early settlers. Since doves are a universal symbol of peace, it's really sad that people don't treat pigeons with more respect.
- Pigeons can memorize as many as three hundred photographs and tell them all apart. They can also associate a glass of water with the ocean.
- Squirrels hang out in parks, too. Like pigeons and starlings, they manage to exist in the trees, drinking from fountains, perhaps, and looking for nuts and leftovers. All these beings have as much (or more) right to be there as we do, so they should be left in peace when we're sharing their space for our recreation.

WHAT YOU CAN DO

- If you see little kids chasing pigeons or startling starlings, try to talk to them—gently. It's not their fault that no one has ever pointed out to them that it's wrong to disturb, harass, or frighten birds or other nonhuman animals. Let them know that pigeons don't mind being watched, from a distance, but that it scares them to be chased. Encourage children to share some of their sandwich with the birds (just the crusts would be appreciated) as a sign of friendship.

- Bird feeding tip: Instead of throwing one or two pieces of bread or crackers at a time, crumble and toss out enough pieces at once and over a large enough area that even the small, young, very old, and clumsy birds will be able to eat without having to fight for a piece.

- Adults, too, may never have thought of their children's actions from the pigeons' point of view, so if the pigeon chaser is too young to understand, ask the parent or guardian to please give the pigeons a break.
- When you go to the park, bring some peanuts (unsalted) in the shell for the squirrels. Put them in the crooks of trees so the squirrels don't have to come down to get them, where they're often chased by dogs and where the nuts could get poisonous things on them.
- When you visit a big park with nature trails, stay on the trails. These trails are like a street out in front of people's homes. When you go off the trails, you invade the privacy of animals who live in the park.
- When you take your dogs to the park, make sure that they are also respectful of the animals who live there. Keep them on leashes or put bells around their necks so other animals can hear them coming.
- Just watching the animals at the park can turn a boring afternoon into an adventure!

CHECK IT OUT

- Call your local **Department of Recreation and Parks** (call Information for the number) to find out if a park ranger can take your class on a tour of a park near you. A park ranger or officer could point out all kinds of plants and animals living in the park— probably a lot more species than you would think!

5 BE SCIENCE FAIR

Which do rats prefer?

A. Maize (Indian corn).
B. Mazes

The answer, of course, is A! Sadly, lots of mice end up in mazes because of old-fashioned "science lessons."

DID YOU KNOW?

- Some pretty grisly and senseless experiments still show up at school science fairs. For example:

  • Students have forced rats to inhale cigarette smoke even though it is well known that smoking is hazardous to human health.
  • A student in Pennsylvania deprived mice of vitamins as a science fair project. Many became frantic and killed each other—some even ate their babies.

• A high school student in California won a prize for cutting out a frog's brain and timing how long the frog could swim around before dying.

• In New York, a student strapped a mouse into a homemade rocket, not thinking about how scared the mouse would be or worrying about injuring or killing him when the rocket lost power and fell back to earth.

● Other students use computer programs, not mice, for their science fair projects. David Liu made a computer model showing how the human brain and eyes work together so we can understand what we see. He won first place in the California State Science Fair and received $40,000!

● You can study nature respectfully. Here are just a few of the things you can learn without harming others:

• Without bats, we might not have bananas. Busy bats pollinate banana trees. You can learn about bats by reading about them.

• Ants have been seen "holding hands" to make a bridge so that others can cross a stream. Study ants by watching a neighborhood ant hill—from a distance.

• Deer only have twins if there's lots of food, and they have no fawns at all if there's a severe food shortage. Read books about how deer control their own populations.

WHAT YOU CAN DO

We don't need to dissect frogs or make rats smoke to understand what their insides look like or to learn that cigarettes are harmful. There are more creative ways to enter the science fair.

● You can make colorful charts that show how the human body works. Study diagrams in encyclopedias and biology books, like *Gray's Anatomy,* to learn about certain parts of the body and how they work together.

● You can observe the land around you. A student named Allen Harker made national news when he studied the beach near his home for more than five years to learn how the waves carry rocks from the mountains to the beach.

- If you'd like to study animals for your science fair project, travel to *their* homes and observe their natural behaviors without interfering.
- Swap the project where you feed rats sugary sweets for one where you count calories and carbohydrates in what *you* eat. You'll learn a lot more!
- Do a science project on animal rights or the environment, maybe on why results from animal tests often don't apply to humans anyway, alternatives to animal testing, or vegetarian nutrition.
- The Animal Welfare Institute suggests observing the squirrels in your neighborhood. If you pay close attention to their behavior and appearance, it won't be long before you are able to identify each one. Note how they chase and play with each other, how they react to birds and other animals, and the time of day they are most active—but resist the urge to interfere with and tame them.

CHECK IT OUT

- Study humans; for example, chart the blood pressure of your classmates. For other projects that help you study yourself, ask your science teacher to call or write **Intellitool,** 1-800-227-3805, Box 459, Batavia, IL 60510-0459, for information on their computer programs "Physiogrip" and "Flexicomp."
- You can contact the **Animal Welfare Institute** at P.O. Box 3650, Washington, DC 20007, to order a copy of their book, *The Endangered Species Handbook*. It costs $6 and is full of ideas on how you can study animals without hurting them. (Or ask your teacher or librarian to order it—they can get it for free.)

6 SAVE THE WHALES

Question: What do whales and rabbits have in common?
Answer: The blue whale's heart is the same size as a Volkswagen Rabbit! The blue whale is the largest animal ever to live on this planet—even bigger than any of the dinosaurs.

DID YOU KNOW?

- Whales communicate with sounds that carry very far underwater. When the ocean is quiet, a whale in Antarctica can hear the call of a whale in Alaska! But because of all the ships and boats on the ocean today, very often whales can't hear each other over long distances anymore. The noise from the motors of our ships must be awful to the whales' sensitive hearing.
- When whales talk to each other it sounds like pings, clicks, and long musical notes to us. The communication between whales is so beautiful that people have recorded it and listen to it as they do other music!

- Whales swim by moving their tails (flukes) up and down. The flukes of humpback whales are as different as people's fingerprints are. Sometimes they bang their flukes on the surface of the water just for fun.
- Whales are mammals and need to breathe air. The blowholes on top of their heads are like our nostrils.
- Baby whales are called calves. Whale calves' aunts often baby-sit them when their mothers have to go somewhere.
- Blue whales can weigh up to 150 tons (that's heavier than ten big school buses), and they can eat one ton of food every day.
- Whales use their flippers for more than just swimming. One mother whale was seen slapping her baby with her flipper to teach him to stay away from a ship.
- Blue whales, along with many other kinds of whales, are following the dinosaurs into the pages of history. They are becoming extinct because people have been killing them and selling their body parts for money. Whale meat is considered a "delicacy" in Japan and some other countries. The oil from their bodies has been used to make lipstick, shoe polish, margarine, and transmission oil for cars and is sometimes used to lubricate weapons. People kill whales with tusks for the same reason they kill elephants for theirs—ivory equals money.
- It is now against the law to kill whales for food anywhere in the world, but Japan and Norway are getting around this law by claiming that they are killing whales to study them. The whales' meat is then sold in stores. People in other places have also been caught killing whales even though it's illegal.

WHAT YOU CAN DO

- Don't buy or accept anything made of ivory. If you receive a gift of ivory, thank your gift giver for the thought but ask them to return the item to the store—and explain why.
- Check lipstick, margarine, and shoe polish for ingredients like "fish oil" or "marine oil," which can come from whales and other sea animals.
- Protest any balloon launches at school fairs and other community events. Balloons often drift into the ocean, where whales and other

sea animals mistake them for food. The balloons get stuck in the animals' insides and can kill them. Chris Palmer wrote a letter to his school principal when he heard about a planned balloon launch. After reading his letter about all the dangers balloons pose to animals in the sea, the principal canceled the launch, and students planted colorful flowers instead. A class of fourth-graders in Connecticut went to their legislators and lobbied for a law to ban balloon launches in that state, and guess what happened? It is now against the law to have balloon launches in Connecticut!

- Avoid going to aquariums and theme parks that keep whales and other sea animals. (See chapter 30, "Born Free, Bored Stiff.")
- Get your class to join you in writing letters to the **Japanese Embassy,** 2520 Massachusetts Ave., N.W., Washington, DC 20008, to ask that Japan leave the whales alone. Let the embassy know that you want whales to be around forever.

CHECK IT OUT

- Write to **The Cousteau Society,** 8440 Santa Monica Blvd., Los Angeles, CA 90069, for more information about whales. You can receive the group's bimonthly newsletter, *Dolphin Log,* written especially for young people, by sending $10 to **The Cousteau Society Membership Center,** 930 West 21st St., Norfolk, VA 23517.
- Write to the **International Fund for Animal Welfare (IFAW),** Box 193, Yarmouth Port, MA 02675, for information about how you can "adopt" a whale.
- Write to the **Sea Shepherd Society,** P.O. Box 7000-S, Redondo Beach, CA 90277, for more information about whales and how you can help them. If you join the group, you receive *The Sea Shepherd Log,* a newsletter describing how the group sinks illegal whaling ships (while no one is on them, of course) to prevent people from killing whales, keeps an eye on tuna companies to try to make them keep their "dolphin-safe" promise, and sails to the North Pole and paints seal babies, which doesn't harm them but makes their fur worthless to people who would otherwise kill them for their coats.

SAVE THE SNAILS

7

If a little bug
Climbs up your arm,
Blow him off gently,
And do him no harm.
—**CHARLIE MARTIN,** age nine

DID YOU KNOW?*

- Snails eat plants with their raspy tongues. They extend their two pairs of feelers by turning them inside out. The longer pair of feelers has eyes at the tips. In dry weather, snails seal themselves into their shells. They can live this way for four years!
- An earthworm has ten hearts.

*Much of this chapter's "Did You Know" information was provided courtesy of the **Marin Humane Society,** 171 Bel Marin Keys Blvd., Novato, CA 94949, and the **Peninsula Humane Society,** Education Department, 12 Airport Blvd., San Mateo, CA 94401.

- Ants live in colonies and are very social. They have highly developed senses of smell and touch. They communicate with their antennae. Ants can lift fifty times their own weight.
- An adult honeybee lives just five weeks.
- Sowbug and pillbug babies emerge from their mother's pouch and ride for a few days under their mother's tail.
- M & M's candies are shiny because they're coated with crushed beetle shells, which are also used to make shellac.
- Nobel Prize winner and famous humanitarian Dr. Albert Schweitzer often stopped to move a worm from the hot pavement to cool dirt.

WHAT YOU CAN DO

- Take time to look closely at small creatures. Sometimes you might try using a magnifying glass or binoculars. Be *very careful* not to touch or move these creatures.
- Imagine yourself in an insect's place.

  • You're standing on a leaf the size of a living room rug and then the wind turns your leaf over.
  • You're a moth emerging from a cramped dark cocoon into a sunlit garden.
  • You, like many butterflies, moths, and other insects, have only a very few days of life. How good it would feel if you were trying to get out of a house through a closed window and someone finally caught you carefully with a drinking glass and a piece of cardboard and released you outside!

- Learn how fascinating insects are. Read books and ask your parents, teacher, and librarian questions about them. Keep a log of your observations.
- Leave insects alone. Each has a place in the environment.
- Help insects if you get a chance. Remember, you can't save them all, but every once in a while a special chance to help one comes along.

• Prop a twig or two in birdbaths so insects who would otherwise drown can climb out. Check the twigs every so often to make sure they're still in place.

• If your porch light fixture has an open bottom, as many do, cover it with a square of aluminum foil held on by a rubber band, so flying bugs won't burn to death on the light bulb.

• If you come upon any injured bugs, give them a merciful death by stepping on them *hard* and quickly. This is kinder than letting them suffer helplessly.

• Help insects inside your home get outside to *their* homes.

● Never throw an insect into the toilet. One woman threw an ant into her toilet and came back later in the day to find him still swimming. She felt terrible, so she rescued him and put him in the yard.

● Respect the rights of small water creatures in and along the banks of ponds, lakes, lagoons, rivers, and oceans to live their short lives without being handled or moved from their homes by people.

● In their *Endangered Species Handbook,* the **Animal Welfare Institute** (P.O. Box 3650, Washington, DC 20007) recommends taking "a field trip to a flower" to observe insects at work.

• Start your studies before the plants bloom or when you first notice some of the flowers. Make a record of the way insects behave in the patch.

• Observe at different times of day, from early growth to full flower to the end of the growing season. Do not disturb the patch in any way that would alter the environment.

● Remember that Dr. Albert Schweitzer said, "No one should be afraid of being laughed at as sentimental. It is the fate of every truth that it shall be a subject for laughter before it is generally recognized." Tell anyone who teases you an interesting fact about bugs, so they will start to appreciate them more.

CHECK IT OUT

- Check out books from your library about insects and small water creatures. Then see if you can see any of the creatures in the book in your own yard.

8

FUR IS UN-FUR-GIVABLE

Question: What do Belinda Carlisle and Barbara Bush have in common?
Answer: They don't wear fur!

Over forty million other-than-human beings are killed every year just because of what they're wearing: fur! Human beings get their "secondhand" fur coats by killing tiny chinchillas, rabbits, beavers, beautiful big cats like lynxes, and lots of other animals. Up to 15 beavers, 25 foxes, 35 raccoons, 40 minks, or 50 muskrats are killed to make just one fur coat!

DID YOU KNOW?

- When the steel-jaw leg-hold trap snaps closed on animals' legs, often breaking them, animals may chew off their own paws to get home to their families, and often they die of hunger or thirst or from struggling. Luckily, the leg-hold trap has been banned in more than seventy countries as well as in Rhode Island, New Jersey, and Florida.

- Other fur-bearing animals live on "ranches." But if that gives you the idea that the animals are lounging around on pillows, forget it! Almost always, the animals never get a chance to feel the ground or play. One young fur farm–raised silver fox who had been kept all her life in a crowded cage was lucky. Fourteen-year-old Kristine Breck saved up $105 and bought "Foxy Lady" at an auction before she could be killed and skinned, giving her a happy home.

- Fur once turned heads, but now it's turning stomachs! Dozens of stores don't sell fur anymore, including **Sears, K mart,** and **Harrods,** the biggest department store in England. Clothes designers like **Bill Blass** refuse to put fur on their dresses and coats; fashion magazines *Mademoiselle, In Fashion,* and *Model* refuse to run fur advertisements; and some of the largest fur companies are going out of business.

- Gentle beavers were once close to extinction because of a demand for beaver hats and collars. Beavers help humans by helping to stop erosion by building dams with their paws and teeth, using mud and tree branches. People trap beavers for fur in underwater traps set outside the lodges where they raise their young and shelter themselves during the winter. Beavers drown in the traps.

- Many famous people refuse to wear fur. Some of them are Jane Wiedlin of the Go-Go's (who recorded the hit song "Fur"), Paul and Linda McCartney, Chrissie Hynde of the Pretenders, Kim Basinger, *Golden Girls'* Rue McClanahan, Ivana Trump, Brooke Shields, Princess Diana of Wales, Ali MacGraw, and Cassandra "Elvira" Peterson.

- Miss Oregon contestant Lisa Verch, a member of Students for the Ethical Treatment of Animals, told the contest organizers in the summer of 1990 that she would not accept a fur coat if she won, even though a mink coat has been the reward for twenty-eight years. She's helping them see that just because it's "tradition" doesn't mean it's right!

- Sarah Gilbert, "Darlene" on ABC's comedy *Roseanne,* says, "It worries me the way we're destroying our environment. We're taking advantage of everything we've got. Fur coats are sometimes just displays of wealth. . . . I don't even like fake furs!"

WHAT YOU CAN DO

- Legendary pioneer Daniel Boone may have worn a raccoon tail hat for warmth, but who can argue for dead animal caps today? Avoid all products made from animals' skins, including teddy bears made of mink and toys like "jumping spiders" made of rabbit fur. Ask for coats made with materials that *don't* harm animals, like fiberfill and Thinsulate. These materials are even warmer than fur and have been worn in Antarctic expeditions and by climbers on snowy Mount Everest.
- Write to **PETA**, P.O. Box 42516, Washington, DC 20015, for free cards that explain why fur production is cruel to animals. When you see people wearing fur coats, hand them a card that starts out, "We'd like you to meet someone who used to wear fur," and has a picture of a fur-bearing animal on it. In department stores, put cards in fur coat pockets.
- If you see furs being bought, sold, or given away in contests, speak up! Write letters, make phone calls, or demonstrate. When a group of students heard that fur was going to be displayed at a reception at their school in Fairfield County, Connecticut, four hundred students signed a petition, which they then circulated. The fur display was canceled.
- If you or a family member has a fur coat, donate it to an animal rights group like PETA. (Your parents will be happy to hear that it is a "tax-deductible donation.") It can be used in displays to teach others *exactly* how fur coats are made. Or check with a local wildlife refuge to see if they'll use furs for orphaned wild animals to snuggle with.

CHECK IT OUT

- For more information on how you can combat the fur industry, contact the **Animal Welfare Institute,** P.O. Box 3650, Washington, DC 20007.
- Order **PETA**'s Fur Action Pack ($15) or Video Fur Action Pack ($25). The Fur Action Pack includes a T-shirt, bumper sticker,

fact sheets, antifur cards, and fliers to start your own antifur campaign. The video pack includes the same, plus an *Exporting Cruelty* video, narrated by Bea Arthur of TV's *Golden Girls*.

- For "Fur Shame" buttons and stickers and a poster that reads "You Should Be Ashamed to Wear Fur," as well as other information, write to the **Humane Society of the United States (HSUS),** 2100 L St., N.W., Washington, DC 20037. The button is $1.00; stickers are $1.50 for twenty-five sheets; and the poster is $2.00.

DON'T PASS THE PRODUCT TESTS

Testing on animals is immoral and cruel—
an animal should never be used as a tool.
So help cruel companies realize
animals have their own interests and lives,
and cruelty-free products are the best buys!
—**GINA SAMSOCK,** age twelve

Until recently, people thought ''animal tests'' meant shampooing rabbits or putting cleansing cream on their whiskers. Of course, it means nothing of the sort. Every year, approximately 14 million animals (more than 38,000 animals every day) are used to test cosmetics, toiletries such as toothpaste and shampoo, and household detergents and other cleaners.

One of the ugliest and, sadly, most common tests on animals is called the Draize test. For this test, liquids, gels, and powders are put into rabbits' eyes, and technicians write down how the eyes react. The animals' eyes can swell, and the animals can even go blind. Acute toxicity tests are even uglier. Often called "lethal dose" tests, they measure the amount of a product it takes to kill part of a group of animals forced to eat it.

Companies that test on animals claim they are protecting people. But despite animal tests, people still get sick from swallowing products, getting them in their eyes, or spilling them on their skin. Testing products on animals seems even crazier when you think about how different our bodies are from a guinea pig's or a rabbit's. Animals used in product tests clearly feel pain, just as we do, but their bodies respond differently to food, drugs, and other products. For example, aspirin helps most human headaches but kills cats—and penicillin kills guinea pigs but can help fight infection in humans.

There are many humane and more accurate ways to make sure the products we use are safe. With encouragement from consumers who refuse to buy products tested on animals, more and more companies are using test tubes, computer programs, human volunteers, artificial human skin, and other methods that don't use animals to make sure the products we use don't harm anybody.

DID YOU KNOW?

- Animal tests are not required by law, and they don't protect us. Other-than-humans' skin and eyes are often very different from ours.
- Companies that don't test on animals use human volunteers, human skin cells grown in laboratories, and other alternatives, as well as known safe and natural ingredients.
- People across the country and around the world are trying to make tests on animals illegal. The two tests mentioned above are *already* against the law in parts of Australia and Italy.
- Over three hundred companies in this country don't test any of their products on animals. Dishwashing liquid and laundry soap made by **Ecover** and **Allen's Naturally** are cruelty-free, and so are cosmetics by **Revlon, Avon,** and **Clinique** and perfumes by **Benetton.**
- Cruel companies make many different products with different names, so watch out! For example, Dry Idea antiperspirant, Paper

Mate pens, Liquid Paper, Silkience shampoo, and numerous other products are made by **Gillette,** a company that refuses to stop using animals.

WHAT YOU CAN DO

- Use only cruelty-free products. It's easy! B-52's singer Kate Pierson uses only cruelty-free hairspray to style her beehive, and it's one of the highest you can find!

  • Write to **PETA,** P.O. Box 42516, Washington, DC 20015, for free lists of hundreds of cruelty-free companies, and share them with your friends.
  • Look for products with PETA's Caring Consumer Product logo. It can only be used by companies that *don't* test on animals.

- Learn how to make your own cruelty-free cleaning products for you and your family to use. With baking soda, salt, vinegar, and other easy-to-find ingredients, you can make dozens of household cleaners. For example, make an effective glass cleaner from white vinegar or rubbing alcohol and water, or a mildew remover from lemon juice and salt. For a list of cleaning recipes, write to **PETA** for the free brochure, "Homemade Household Product Recipes."
- Instead of buying a birthday present for a parent's next birthday, offer to clean the house! Use cruelty-free products, or make your own.
- Whatever your chores, use cruelty-free products to do them. Make your own bathroom cleaner, or get your parents to buy laundry detergent not tested on animals, such as PETA's brand, Choice. (Write to **PETA Merchandise,** P.O. Box 42400, Washington, DC 20015, for a free catalog.)
- Take inventory. If you have cruel products in your home cabinets, ask your parents if you can mail them back to the companies that made them (try sending the package C.O.D., meaning the receiver pays the postage). Tell the companies you disagree with animal tests and find their product *unsatisfactory*. Some companies may send you a refund. Here's a sample letter:

President
Johnson & Johnson
1 Johnson & Johnson Plaza
New Brunswick, NJ 08933

Dear President,

I am returning this bottle of Tide detergent because I find it unsatisfactory now that I know your company uses animal tests. Until you stop testing on animals, my family won't buy any more Johnson & Johnson products. Instead, we will buy cruelty-free cleaning products from companies like Ecover, PETA, and Allen's Naturally. Please send me a full refund, and please stop testing on animals.

Very disappointed,
[your name]

- Be a positive nuisance. James Sexton, a teenager from New York, spent a day handing out leaflets in front of a store that sold perfume that had been tested on animals. By six that evening, the manager had pulled the perfume from the shelves.

CHECK IT OUT

- Write to **PETA** for a free color catalog of cruelty-free household products and toiletries.
- A free catalog of cruelty-free household products is also available from **Allen's Naturally,** P.O. Box 339, Department A, Farmington, MI 48332-0514.
- Free catalogs of cruelty-free cosmetics are available from:

  - **Compassion Cosmetics,** P.O. Box 3534, Glendale, CA 91201.
  - **Colour Quest,** 616 Third St., St. Charles, IL 60174.

● For a catalog and *free samples* of cruelty-free cosmetics, write to **Lion & Lamb, Inc.**, 29-28 41st Ave., Suite 813A, Long Island City, NY 11101.

10 | HORSING AROUND

Horse sense is what keeps horses from betting on what people will do.
—**RAYMOND NASH**

One kid said to another, "I went riding this morning."

"Horseback?" asked his friend.

"Yup, he got back before I did."

In some places in the United States, such as Nevada and New Mexico, you can still see groups of wild horses running free across meadows, kicking up dirt, courting, eating a variety of different kinds of grasses and shrubs, playing, and raising their families.

Wild horses are being pushed off the land they need to survive because cattle ranchers want to take away the wild horses' right to eat wild grasses. The ranchers would rather use the grass to fatten up their cattle, and they have convinced the government to round up many of the horses and auction them off. More than ninety thousand wild horses have been rounded up since 1973! Lots of these end up being killed for dog food.

On an island called Assateague, off the coast of Virginia, wild horses are chased across a river in the middle of summer every year, and their babies are sold to anyone who will pay for them. Many of the ponies aren't yet old enough to live without their mothers, and the people who buy them often don't know how to take care of a growing pony.

DID YOU KNOW?

- In Australia, friends are called "cobbers." A "cob" is a small horse, usually a stout and solid one.
- Horses are closely related to zebras.
- Wild horses live in groups called "harems" made up of several females and one stallion. Harems are very close knit family groups.
- Can you understand "horse"? Horses communicate by whinnying, neighing, and making other sounds with different tones and patterns. Horses nuzzle and rub their heads on people and horses they trust. When certain Eskimos meet they rub noses, but when horses greet each other they sometimes put their noses together and blow into each other's nostrils! Horses in love stay close to each other. When they are afraid or think they may have to fight, horses rear up on their hind legs. They put their ears back flat when they are upset, and their eyes tell a million stories about the way they feel.

WHAT YOU CAN DO

- Write to your congressperson (**United States House of Representatives,** Washington, DC 20510) asking that no more money be given to the Bureau of Land Management for wild horse roundups. (If you don't know the name of your congressperson, ask your librarian.) Tell your representative that you don't want ranchers kicking wild horses and other animals out of their home ranges. Explain that the land where the horses are being rounded up is public property belonging to all of us, and that the lives of horses are more important than life*less* hamburgers. (See chapter 29 for tips on letter writing.)

- People are trying to get the horrible roundups stopped. You can help by writing a letter of protest to the **Refuge Manager,** Chincoteague NWR, P.O. Box 62, Chincoteague, VA 23336. Your letter might look something like this one:

Dear Refuge Manager,

I just learned about the wild pony roundup. I am writing to ask you to stop catching these frightened ponies and auctioning them off to whoever comes along. I love horses, but would never buy one who was taken away from her mother and sold against her will.

I am also upset about how the ponies are forced to swim across the channel from Assateague Island. I think this is mean and could hurt the horses.

I know the fire department needs to raise money to keep going, but there are a *lot* of other ways to do it. The horses should be allowed their freedom.

Please stop the roundup and auction, and please don't write back and tell me it's okay, because it *isn't.*

Sincerely,
[Your name]

- Take up a collection for **Black Beauty Ranch** in Murchison, Texas, where wild horses find safety (address under "Check It Out"). The ranch has adopted many wild horses after they were rounded up unfairly by the Bureau of Land Management, and the horses now roam freely on more than six hundred natural acres! Black Beauty Ranch has become a sanctuary for all kinds of animals.
- When Melissa Sanders visited the "kiddie rides" at the town fair and saw ponies forced to walk in circles for hours in the hot sun, she was upset. But when she saw that the ponies were so skinny that their saddles didn't fit properly, she was *angry*! After she left the fair, Melissa wrote a letter to the fair organizers, the mayor of her town, and the editors of her local newspapers. Melissa has

made a vow that next year she will be ready with leaflets she made up to hand out all over town. She also has the number of the local humane society on hand for when she visits the fair. She says, "People can't just do whatever they want to animals so that they can make money. I won't let them get away with being mean to the ponies again."

● Help stop horse-and-buggy rides, which aren't as fun and romantic as they look. Tell people about how these horses can pound the pavement all day long in the summer heat, pulling buggies full of people through heavy traffic. If carriage-horse rides are offered in your town, write a letter of protest to the mayor or call the mayor's office. (Go to your local library for the mayor's name and address.)

● Avoid riding stables even if you *can* stay on. It can't be fun to have a different stranger on your back every hour of the day, especially when many of them don't know how to ride gently and yank on the reins, pull on the bit in your mouth, and kick you in the ribs.

● Bring carrots and apples to horses kept in stalls and fields. They love getting delicious treats to break up the boring day. Check the condition of the horses, too. Are their hooves cracked, overgrown, and dry, or shiny and trimmed? Are their coats dull and dry or shiny and soft? Are the horses nice and round or too skinny? If they seem sick or neglected, ask the local humane society to come and check on them.

● Don't go to horse races. They can be exciting for people but miserable for horses. When horses are injured or their feet hurt, people sometimes give them drugs to numb the pain—but make them keep racing. This makes their injuries even worse. Try to get your school to put on a "race against horse racing." Have three-legged races, sack races, and/or human wheelbarrow races, and invite the whole town to come and watch or join in. Ask for a donation at the door and send the money you collect to your favorite horse protection group.

CHECK IT OUT

- Send a self-addressed, stamped envelope to **Black Beauty Ranch,** P.O. Box 367, Murchison, TX 75778, for more information about the ranch and the animals they have saved.
- Write for information or join the **Hooved Animal Humane Society (HAHS),** P.O. Box 1099, Woodstock, IL 60089. HAHS rescues abused and neglected horses and rehabilitates them in a sanctuary until they can be adopted into good homes. HAHS has sixty of its own investigators. The **Indiana Hooved Animal Humane Society,** P.O. Box 500, Morocco, IN 47963, does many of the same things.

11 CHICKEN OUT

I stopped eating chickens
When I was only eight
I'd rather Henny had a life
Than lay here on my plate!
—GABRIELLE MARTIN, age thirteen

DID YOU KNOW?

- Butterscotch, a little hen in Woodstock, Illinois, loved people so much, she would run down the farm's dirt road to meet visitors. Then she would hop up and down at their feet until they picked her up and cuddled her in their arms.
- Lucie, a rooster (in spite of his name), lives with a family in Great Neck, New York. Lucie stands on a chair at the dinner table with them and eats from a plate. He's always checking to see if people have something on their plate that he doesn't have. He loves to be with people. If they raise their voices, he chimes in so loudly

that it's impossible to shout over him, and everyone winds up laughing.

- Gonzo, a rooster, was given to children as an Easter gift. When he grew up nobody wanted him, so someone fed him poison. When that didn't kill him, someone wrung his neck and put him in a garbage can, where he almost froze to death. A garbage man rescued him and gave him to a kind person. For a long time Gonzo could only give raspy gurgles; but after six months Gonzo finally crowed again, and in his good new home he lived to a very old age.

- Hens and their chicks talk to each other even while the chicks are still inside their eggshells. Hens make at least eleven different peeps and clucks to talk to their chicks for as much as two days before the chicks hatch.

- Why did the chicken stop in the middle of the road? To lay it on the line! Today, billions of chickens never get outside—they live inside dark, smelly egg factories. They spend their whole lives jammed into cages so small, they can't even stretch a wing. Their bodies get sores on them as they try to turn around. When they lay an egg, it rolls away on a conveyor belt.

- In the time it takes you to read this page, approximately five thousand chickens will have been killed for U.S. tables.

- Because billions of chickens are raised in huge, dirty factories, eating chicken causes millions of cases of stomach flu each year.

- Turkeys, geese, and ducks are also interesting individuals and are better as friends than as holiday dinners! They, too, suffer because people wrongly think of them as dumb and unimportant.

WHAT YOU CAN DO

- Learn to appreciate chickens and other domestic birds for the wonderful individuals they are. Realize that each has his or her own special personality and feelings.

- When you hear other people refer to chickens, turkeys, or ducks in a mean or thoughtless way, tell them that these delightful animals deserve good treatment. Tell them about Butterscotch, Lucie, Gonzo and any other chickens you may know. You can help change people's attitudes.

- Tell people baby chicks aren't toys to be given as Easter gifts. Write a letter to your local newspaper two weeks or so before Easter, telling readers why they shouldn't give chicks as gifts. Your letter can be as simple as this:

Editor
Daily News
4 Main Street
Mytown, VT

Dear Editor,

It's mean and wrong to give or sell chicks for Easter. They are fragile and innocent. People don't know how to take care of them. Some people are very cruel to them.

Sincerely,
Amanda Jones

- Don't buy anything with real feathers. Usually chickens or other animals had to die to provide them. If you have a feather pillow or comforter, buy a nonfeather one when it wears out.
- Try interesting, delicious, nutritious vegetarian foods in place of chicken, turkey, geese, ducks, and eggs. If you still like the taste of chicken, you can buy nonanimal substitutes that taste the same and are better for you. **Worthington** makes "Crispy Chik" patties, "FriChik" cutlets, and other chicken-style fake meats.
- Do a report on the wonderful qualities of chickens.

CHECK IT OUT

- Check your library for more true stories about chickens and other domestic birds.
- Read about the sad ways millions of chickens and turkeys are raised for meat and eggs. **PETA** can send you information, or write to **Farm Animal Rangers,** Compassion in World Farming,

20 Lavant St., Petersfield, Hampshire GU32 3EW, England. Be sure to ask FAR for a copy of the poster, "Lifesize Hen in Living Space Allowed to Her."

• For information about the factory farming of chickens, and for tips on helping put an end to it, write to **Chickens's Lib**, P.O. Box 2, Holmsfirth, Huddersfield, HD7 1QT, England.

12 | IT'S RAINING CATS AND DOGS

ANYBODY HAVE A CALCULATOR?

Question: If 6 cats have 6 kittens every 6 months, and each of those kittens has 6 kittens every 6 months, how many cats would you have after 6 years?

Answer: 2,176,772,336!! That's equal to more than a third of the world's population of people.

The number of homeless animals is more than we can imagine: twenty million dogs and cats who enter animal shelters every year in the United States never find a home. Yet pet shop suppliers and other people keep breeding even more cats and dogs—that's like putting gasoline on a fire that's already out of control!

DID YOU KNOW?

- Three to five thousand puppies and kittens are born every hour in the United States. For every person who comes into the world, fifteen dogs and forty-five cats are also born.
- Animal shelters and pounds take in twenty-seven million lost or abandoned dogs and cats every year.

WHAT YOU CAN DO

- Have female cats and dogs spayed and males neutered (or "altered") so they won't have puppies or kittens. Both operations are pretty simple and very safe. They also prevent some health problems and make animals less likely to wander off in search of a mate. Dogs and cats should be spayed or neutered as soon as possible—at about six months of age—so that they won't add to the overpopulation problem. Every litter hurts because every home you find for the new puppies or kittens is a home taken away from an animal in a shelter.

CHECK IT OUT

- Chances are, your local animal shelter has leaflets you can distribute to encourage spaying and neutering. If not, write for free fliers to **PETA**, P.O. Box 42516, Washington, DC 20015.
- Many humane society shelters sponsor low-cost or free spay/neuter services. If you can't find such a program near you, call the **Friends of Animals'** toll-free, low-cost spay/neuter hot line, 1-800-631-2212.

13 "COMPANIMALS"* ARE PRICELESS

KID: Mom, can we get a dog?
MOM: I don't know, Junior; they cost $25 apiece.
KID: But, Mom, I want a whole one!

"How much is that doggie in the window?" Don't ask! If you and your family decide to bring an animal into your home, adopt one (or two) from a shelter. That way you can save a homeless animal from death, and your money won't be used to support the dog and cat population explosion.

The goal of pet shops is to make money, so animals in them are often treated as just another "item" to be sold. This means many of them are not well cared for: they go without the love, care, and attention they need to grow up healthy in body and spirit.

---

*"Companimals" is short for "companion animals"—a more loving and respectful term for the animals many people call "pets."

DID YOU KNOW?

- "Puppy mills" in the Midwest supply pet shops with most of their dogs. In these places mother dogs and their litters usually live in small, outdoor cages, with wire mesh bottoms that make walking uncomfortable.
- Because of their difficult beginnings, animals from puppy mills can develop behavior problems. Puppy mill "purebred" dogs sold to pet shops also often have physical problems, like weak legs, because of overbreeding and inbreeding. Purebred dogs are mixtures of other dogs bred by people who wanted dogs with short noses, long legs, or barrel chests.
- To get certain looks for hunting, fighting, or showing off, some people still cut ("crop") the ears of certain dogs like Dobermans and cut off ("dock") dogs' tails.
- "Mutts" don't have the problems purebreds do and are no less special.
- The "fancy" animals sold at pet stores may be pretty, but the story behind them probably isn't! For every exotic bird (that is, one not native to this country) you see in the store, four others died during their capture or transport to the United States. They, and other exotic animals like lizards and snakes, usually don't live very long when they get to the United States because they come from tropical forests or deserts where the climate and the food supply are very different.
- Some pet shops also sell animals who aren't exotic but are not usually domesticated, such as turtles, fishes, prairie dogs, and ferrets. More and more breeders are getting into the act as well, selling animals such as minipigs and llamas as trendy companions. Once in people's homes, these animals can easily suffer because their guardians don't know exactly how to care for them.

WHAT YOU CAN DO

- Purchase leashes, toys, and other supplies for companion animals at supply stores that don't sell animals.

- Animals belong in their natural habitats, so never buy a caged bird, exotic animal, or trendy companion animal. Protest the sale of animals like these with complaints, letters, or a demonstration (or all three).
- The **Animal Welfare Institute** suggests that you:

  • Visit pet stores in your area and make lists of the wild animals being sold. If you find an endangered bird, reptile, or other animal, immediately contact the nearest office of the **U.S. Fish and Wildlife Service** to report it. There is a list of endangered species in the Animal Welfare Institute's *Endangered Species Handbook* ($6, postage paid).
  • Check the store for cleanliness and see whether you think the animals are healthy. If the cages are dirty or if the animals have dull coats or seem very tired, write or call your local humane society and the **Animal and Plant Health Inspection Service,** U.S. Department of Agriculture, Washington, DC 20782. The Animal Welfare Institute would also like to hear about your investigation. (See address below.)

- Don't buy tropical or other fishes; like birds, fishes are accustomed to living in groups and having a lot of space in which to move about.
- When you are ready to adopt an animal, don't overlook dogs or cats who may not seem "cute" to other people. Old, weird-looking, and even scruffy animals need love just as much as any others.

CHECK IT OUT

- Write to **PETA,** P.O. Box 42516, Washington, DC 20015, for a free fact sheet on what other things to look for in your local pet store.
- For information on the exotic bird trade, order a copy of *The Bird Business* by Greta Nilsson from the **Animal Welfare Institute,** P.O. Box 3650, Washington, DC 20007; the cost is $5 (postage paid).

14 PEN PALS FOR ANIMALS

Question: What did the envelope say to the mail carrier?
Answer: Stamp out animal cruelty!

DID YOU KNOW?

- People all over the country—and all over the world—care about animals: from Athens, Georgia, to Athens, Greece; from Paris, Texas, to Paris, France; and from Venice, California, to Venice, Italy!
- Some animal protection groups can put you in touch with new friends both close to home and far, far away.
- You can learn a lot from your pen pal(s). You'll be able to swap stories and ideas, even share recipes.
- Overseas pen pals can keep you updated on animal protection in their countries, and you'll be able to help by writing letters in behalf of animals in other countries.

WHAT YOU CAN DO

● Write a letter about yourself.

• Do you live with any other-than-human beings? Tell about them—their names, their ages, how you met them, and what they're like.
• Do you have any hobbies? Do you play sports? Do you collect anything?
• What kind of music do you like to listen to? What kinds of books do you like to read? Do you like to paint or draw?
• What are your favorite subjects in school?
• Describe the area where you live.
• What do you do to help animals? Are you in a club? Are you a vegetarian? If so, what's your favorite dish?

● Send your letter to one of the groups listed below.

CHECK IT OUT

● Write to **PETA Kids,** P.O. Box 42516, Washington, DC 20015, to get a list of kids enrolled in their pen pal program. You can pick the pen pals you want to write to. Send a letter about yourself and ask to be included in the next pen pal listing.
● You can make an overseas friend by sending a letter (with an airmail stamp or two regular stamps on it) about yourself to:

• **Scribble Line,** Animal Aid Youth Group, 7 Castle St., Tonbridge, Kent TN9 1BH, England.
• **Greenscene,** The Vegetarian Society, Parkdale, Dunham Rd., Altrincham, Cheshire, WA14 4QG, England. *Greenscene* will print part of your letter, and you could get lots of responses!
• **Pen Pal Link-up,** Compassion in World Farming, 20 Lavant St., Petersfield, Hampshire GU32 3EW, England. To join Pen Pal Link-up, you need to be a member of Farm Animal Rangers. Send

£2 (that's British pounds, about $4) to receive badges, stickers, FAR's magazine, *OUT,* and information on the pen pal program.

● The **Animal Welfare Institute** has a list of groups you can contact to find a pen pal who shares your concern for endangered species. Write to a student overseas about an endangered species in his or her country. If you can, write your letter in the language of the country. Tell your pen pal about a U.S.–endangered species and the need to protect its members. Ask your pen pals to write to you about threatened or endangered species in their countries.

• Simon Muchiru of the **Wildlife Clubs of Kenya** writes: "The African wildlife is nature's gift to mankind, part of the world's heritage. Some of the wildlife is now endangered or threatened with extinction. The young people of Africa are committed to saving it. They would like to share the information on these animals with you.

"There are wildlife clubs in several English- and French-speaking countries in Africa in primary schools through university colleges. If you would like to share information on endangered species of Africa, you can get a pen pal through the wildlife clubs. I can help you get in touch with these clubs in Africa. If you wish to do so, please write to me and I will help you wherever I can. They would also love to know about your wildlife.

"My address is **Environmental Liaison Center,** P.O. Box 72461, Nairobi, Kenya."

• The following people and organizations should also be able to put you in touch with a pen pal who cares about protecting endangered species:

1. Sra. Anna Chaves Quiroz, **Programa de Educación Ambiental,** Universidad Estatal a Distancia, Apdo. 2, Plaza Gonzalez Viquez, San Jose, Costa Rica.

2. Sr. Julio Jaen, **Asociación Estudiantil para la Conservación Ambiental,** c/o Smithsonian Tropical Research Institute, APO, Miami, FL 34002.

3. Erika Sela, Julian Hernandez 8, Madrid 33, Spain.

4. Beauty Without Cruelty, c/o Ms. Jean Meade, 112 Aberdeen Place, Whangamata, New Zealand.

5. Frederic Henry, **Animaux Informations Jeunes,** B.P. 74 35403, Saint-Malo Cedex, France.

15 WATCH OUT FOR ANIMALS

When Abraham Lincoln made his driver stop so he could put a baby bird back in her nest, his friends made fun of him—but he told them, "I could not have slept tonight it I had left that helpless little creature to perish on the ground."

When Lauren and Michael Cohn saw some neighborhood kids using slingshots to shoot birds and squirrels in the woods near their house, they took action. They let their parents know what was going on right away, and together they drove the slingshot users out of the woods. Then they formed a Neighborhood Animal Watch. In the past year, their group has saved birds and a baby rabbit from the mouths of wandering cats, found a new home for an old cat abandoned by his family when they moved, taken a dog found with BB gunshot in him to a veterinarian, put baby birds safely back in their nests, called for help for animals hit by cars, and put food out at night for raccoons and rabbits and food out on winter days for birds and squirrels.

DID YOU KNOW?

● Caring kids like Lauren and Michael first invented the Neighborhood Animal Watch to take care of animal emergencies, like birds falling from nests. Now the watches are in neighborhoods all over the United States.

● A ship's crew usually keeps four-hour watches, but two-hour watches are called "dog watches."

WHAT YOU CAN DO

● Set up a neighborhood meeting for kids who care about animals.

   • Post notices of the meeting at your neighborhood school, supermarkets, and libraries.
   • Go door to door with fliers. (Your newspaper carrier might help.)
   • Choose a name for your group. You could even have a special password, hand sign, or animal call.

● At the meeting, have everyone think of past animal emergencies. What went right and what went wrong? Write down all the helpful tips and make a list of problems to solve.

   • The kids in Lauren and Michael's Neighborhood Animal Watch have learned a lot about animals and how to help them. They know, for example, that wild animals can go into shock just from being held by humans. They found out that, as neat as it is to be around them, staring at animals and stroking them can fill them with so much fear that it kills them. "The most important thing to do when you find an injured animal is to get him into a box with air holes and a blanket or other warm material as quickly as possible. Otherwise, he could be scared to death," says Michael.

● Make a list of numbers to call for help with animals who are lost, found, hurt, or being mistreated or who need homes, and give it to everyone in your neighborhood. (Your local humane society can probably give you these numbers.) Your list should look something like this:

KINDNESS CLUB NEIGHBORHOOD ANIMAL WATCH

1. SMITH COUNTY HUMANE SOCIETY: 111 Walton Road; 555-2224. Lost dogs and cats (only) picked up; Mon.–Fri., 3–5 P.M. Will take in animals Mon.–Sat. until 9 P.M. Has low-cost spay/neuter program.
2. SMITH COUNTY POLICE DEPT.: after-hours pickup of injured animals; 555-6084.
3. DR. JONES, EMERGENCY VET: 555-2471 until 5 P.M., 555-7082 after 5 P.M.
4. BIRDS: Jenny Adams, 555-4119 or 555-4075*** or Gary Fisher, 359-0088.
5. WILDLIFE: Mark Johnson (all), 555-9996**** or Trudy Marshall (squirrels only), 555-9075.
6. OTHER ADULTS who will help when needed:
    Carol Anderson, 555-2256*
    John Brown, 555-1239**
    James Thompson, 555-4455*
    Marcia Malone, 555-9976*****
    Kim Talbot, 555-6789*
Add more names as you get them. Make sure they are people who really care.)

*Has holding place for dog
**Has holding place for cat
***Has holding place for bird
****Has holding place for wild creature
*****Has holding place during weekdays

● Educate your community about animals. Make a poster of your list, including pictures of all the kinds of animals living in your community, and put a copy of it in every neighborhood mailbox. Michael and Lauren's group did this and have found that most people do want to help animals once they find out that they can. "A lot of people just give up when they see an animal on the side of the road or injured in their yard," says Lauren. "They figure that there's nothing they can do to help. We tell them that there is a *lot* they can do for animals, and now our community is animal active!"

● Here's how to handle an injured animal:

• Someone should stay with an injured animal while someone else calls for professional help.

• Be careful! A dog, cat, or wild animal can bite when hurt. Use heavy gloves and a blanket when approaching them.

• You can calm wild animals by placing large cardboard boxes over them. (First punch air holes in the box.)

• Baby birds who are just learning to fly are often out practicing with their mothers in the spring. Leave baby birds alone. Their mothers are almost always nearby or getting food for them. If you find a baby bird who is injured, or is still alone after sundown, put him or her gently into a little box with air holes punched in it and call a wildlife rehabilitator, a person licensed to take care of injured and orphaned wild creatures. Knowing that wild animals who trust people will later be in danger from people who might want to harm them, the rehabilitator helps them learn to get along again on their own and, when they're healthy, releases them in a protected area. To find out if there's a wildlife rehabilitator in your area, call your local humane society, park district, or veterinarian.

• Injured dogs or cats may feel better if someone puts a blanket over them and talks softly.

• If an animal needs to be moved, *be very gentle*. Depending upon the animal and the injury, you might use a board, a heavy jacket, a blanket, or a car mat. Try to get an adult to help.

• If the animal is in the road, make sure you get an adult to help you. Run to a nearby house and/or flag down a motorist. Do not risk your own safety by standing in the road. (For more details, see chapter 49.)

● Distribute seasonal "alert" fliers that remind people about proper animal care. Tell your community:

• straw is better than blankets in doghouses during winter. (Blankets can get wet and freeze.)

• not to leave animals in a car on a hot day, and why (see chapter 37).

• some things they can do to control fleas, such as flea-combing and vacuuming frequently, as well as adding brewer's yeast and garlic to their companion animals' food.

● Adopt a shut-in. Is there a lonely dog living in a backyard in your neighborhood? Dogs need love and companionship. Neighborhood "Watchdogs" can try getting permission to walk lonely dogs and to sit or play with them. Once you start, don't break their hearts by not coming back (see chapter 1 for dogs' needs).

• Do the dogs have doghouses that protect them from the weather? They should be:

1. up against the humans' house, not out in the middle of nowhere
2. made of wood
3. set off the ground a few inches
4. facing south
5. in a shady spot in summer
6. filled with straw
7. equipped with a door flap to keep out wind and snow in winter.

• Make sure:

1. the dogs have fresh water in a tip-proof bucket, and that the water's not frozen in the winter.
2. they are being fed properly.
3. they are not ill (if they seem especially weak, are bleeding anywhere, have a cough, or otherwise seem sick, get help).
4. the chain or rope (if they're tied up) can't get tangled around things like bushes, trees, chairs, and the like.
5. their collars aren't cutting into their necks (remember, three of your fingers should fit under the collar).

• Find out if the dogs are spayed or neutered—the last thing a forgotten dog needs is a whole family of forgotten dogs!

- If any of these things needs attention, politely ask the dog's guardians to fix them, or fix them yourself, with permission. If they don't and won't let you, call your local humane society for help.
- How to handle stray animals:

  • When you find strays, put them in a safe place until their real home can be found. If you can, bring them to your house, giving them food, water, attention, and bedding. If you can't take care of them, ask a friend to, or check your Neighborhood Animal Watch list to see who can. As a last resort, take them to the local shelter, and check up on them often until you find their real guardian—or a good new one.
  • Call in a "found report" to your animal shelters and local newspapers. Many newspapers will run a free "found" ad. Since someone could pretend to be an animal's guardian and then sell him or her to a laboratory for experiments, don't give out details about the animal in the ad. Instead, have the person who calls do the describing.

- When animals need new homes, be careful! They are counting on you to find a home where they will be permanently cared for and loved.

  • Don't give an animal to anyone you have doubts about. Wait for another home you know will be loving.
  • If the animal can't be spayed or neutered before the adoption, be sure the new guardian signs an agreement that it will be done. Sample agreements are available from PETA.
  • If you run out of time, it is kinder to take animals to a well-run shelter than to give them to not-so-good homes.

CHECK IT OUT

- Write to PETA for a free brochure on helping injured baby birds and for these free fact sheets that will help make everyone an expert "Watchdog":

  - "Procedures for a Cruelty Investigation"
  - "Guide to the Sale & Giveaway of Companion Animals"
  - "How to Trap Animals Humanely"
  - "Animal Shelters: Hope for the Homeless"
  - "Flea Control: Safe Solutions"
  - "Spaying & Neutering: A Solution for Suffering"
  - "Declawing Cats: Manicure or Mutilation?"

16 DUMP WASTEFUL HABITS

A piece of school notebook paper takes thirty days and thirty nights to break down into pieces small enough to become part of the earth again! Can you guess how long a soda can takes to decompose?

A. Two years.
B. Twenty years.
C. Two hundred years.

Letter C is correct! If our great-great-great-great-great-grandparents had used soda cans, we'd be knee deep in them (the cans, not our ancestors) today.

DID YOU KNOW?

- One Thanksgiving, Mary Beth Sweetland saw a duck whose beak was caught in a plastic six-pack holder. The six-pack holder made it impossible for him to eat. Mary Beth had to work hard to win his trust. Every day for two weeks she coaxed him ashore with soothing words and cracked corn. Finally, "Mr. Quackster" came close enough for Mary Beth and a friend to snip the plastic ring—freeing the duck from litter that would have taken his life. As he flew away, Mary Beth says all she could do was sit on the bank and cry with joy.

- A dead sea turtle was found with enough plastic garbage in her stomach to carpet the floor of a large room. Turtles often mistake plastic for food and can die when it clogs their stomachs.
- Littering is costly to all of us. Litter pickup and disposal in our nation's parks costs $15 million a year—enough to buy a Nintendo game for every single person in Tucson, Arizona.

WHAT YOU CAN DO

It causes problems at home when we make a mess. When we mess up the planet, the problems multiply and affect millions of animals.

- Hope Buyukmihci, who runs the **Unexpected Wildlife Refuge,** asks us to imagine how we'd feel if we stepped on broken glass with bare feet or got our noses stuck in the openings of soda cans.
- Why not organize a litter pickup? Get your family, friends, and neighbors to help you. Each person should carry a sturdy bag for collecting cans, bottles (be careful of broken glass), papers, and gum and candy wrappers (are any yours?) along the road, in the woods, or around a pond. If you do it every fourth Saturday, you could pick a different site each month.
- Organize litter patrols along creeks and streams, in meadows, and on the street. And, whether you're walking to school or tromping through the woods, keep an eye out for—and always pick up—cans, wrappers, six-pack rings, and so on. Recycle what you can!
- Start a recycling program at home and at school. Most recycling centers take newspapers, aluminum cans, and glass. Many now take plastic and metal food cans as well. Look in the Yellow Pages under "Recycling Centers" for one near you. Or call the **Environmental Defense Fund**'s recycling hot line to receive information about recycling in your area: 1-800-CALL-EDF.
- Before throwing away or recycling plastic six-pack rings, snip each ring.

- Rinse out empty metal food containers well and smash the open end closed so small animals can't get their heads caught in them.
- Try to use everything over and over before you throw it away. Bring plastic and paper grocery bags back to the store with you every time you shop. Use them until they fall apart! Better yet, buy or macramé a string mesh or canvas bag you can use all the time. Cotton string bags from **Seventh Generation,** Colchester, VT 05446, cost $8.95 for two. They make great gifts!
- Have a yard sale. Sell your old things that you don't want anymore because one person's junk is another's treasure! What you can't sell, give away.
- Start a compost pile in your backyard for organic garbage like food scraps, coffee grounds, and grass clippings. This kind of "garbage" turns back into dirt full of nutrients to feed the Earth. Luckily, one quarter of all our garbage is organic waste!

CHECK IT OUT

- Write to **Defenders of Wildlife,** 1244 19th St., N.W., Washington, DC 20036, for their free article, "The Trashy Sea Around Us," for more information on how garbage can hurt animals.
- Subscribe to *P3, The Earth-Based Magazine for Kids,* P.O. Box 52, Montgomery, VT 05470. Subscriptions cost $18. Or send $2 for a sample copy and ask for the Sept./Oct. 1990 "garbage" issue.
- Send $2.50 to **Earth Care Paper Company,** 325 Beech Lane, Harbor Springs, MI 49740, for a copy of the booklet *The Art of Composting,* which is full of ideas for turning garbage into environmental gold.
- For information on how your school can compost cafeteria leftovers, write to the **Division of Solid Waste Management,** Agency of Natural Resources, 103 S. Main St., West Building, Waterburg, VT 05676. Ask for the cafeteria composting guidelines.
- Be a part of a beach cleanup, usually held in the fall. For information, write to the **Coastal States Organization,** c/o Margie Fleming, 444 N. Capitol St., N.W., Suite 312, Washington, DC 20001; or the **Center for Environmental Education,** 1725 DeSales St., N.W., Washington, DC 20036.

- Write to the **Environmental Defense Fund,** 1616 P St., N.W., Washington, DC 20036, for ideas on how you can help keep garbage to a minimum and for an Earth Day reading list divided into three age groups, from preschool through sixth grade.
- Watch TBS television's *Captain Planet* cartoon series starring a superhero who works to save the Earth. The twenty-six-episode series started in September 1990.

17 FREE THE FISHES

Enjoy thy stream, O harmless fish:
And when an angler for his dish.
  Through gluttony's vile sin,
Attempts, a wretch, to pull thee out,
God give thee strength, O gentle trout,
To pull the rascal in!
        —**JOHN WOLCOT** (1738–1819)
          from *The Neighbours: An Animal Anthology*

We've all heard that fishes are smart because they live in schools. Well, some fishes are *so* smart that they've come up with truly clever ways to hide their babies when they sense danger. Guess where mother cichlid fishes hide their babies:

A. In a snorkel.
B. On a boat.
C. In their mouths.

  Letter C is correct. Some fishes open wide and let their babies swim right inside their mouths if a big fish comes after them. Other father fishes, such as cardinal fishes, actually carry the eggs that hold their babies in their mouths until they hatch!

DID YOU KNOW?

- The first hitchhikers were fishes called "remoras," or "suckerfishes." These fishes actually "hitch rides" with sharks and other large sea animals by attaching the sucking disk (sort of like the plastic suction cups you attach to windows) on top of their heads to the underside of the shark.
- Fishes never close their eyes.
- Fishes use their mouths for many things that people do with their hands: collecting food, building homes, and taking care of their babies. As a result, their mouths are very sensitive, so fishes get badly hurt when caught on hooks. Even if the fishes are thrown back into the water, their lips are wounded and can become infected.
- John Bryant, author of *Fettered Kingdoms*, says that the three things needed for fishing are "a hook, a line, and a stinker!"
- Fishes can be very compassionate. A South African magazine reported a true story about a deformed goldfish named Blackie and his friend Big Red. Blackie had trouble swimming, and for over a year Big Red kept constant watch over his sick friend, gently carrying him on his back and swimming him around the tank. Every day, at feeding time, Big Red picked Blackie up and swam to the water surface where they both ate together.
- Some people think fishing is a relaxing way to spend a day, but it certainly isn't relaxing for the fishes! Most people don't realize that fishes *do* feel pain.
- Frenchman Alphonse Alais invented a frosted fish tank for shy fishes.
- Careless people often litter lakes and streams with fishing line. Egrets, ducks, fishes, muskrats, possums, and other animals who come to the water for a drink get tangled and sometimes strangled in this sharp plastic string.

WHAT YOU CAN DO

- If someone asks you to go fishing, explain why you won't go. Tell them that fishes have feelings and deserve to live just like anyone else. Suggest a game of "Go Fish" with cards or going bird or fish *watching* (but not disturbing) instead.
- Organize litter patrols along streams and lakes to clean up fishing line and other dangerous litter (watch out for hooks) left by people who fish. Put up signs reading "Please do not leave fishing line here."
- If your school carnival or fair has contests that give free goldfishes as prizes, organize a group of students to complain to the principal. Explain that a frightened, lonely goldfish is no prize, and suggest plush animal toys or other prizes instead.
- Don't buy tropical fishes or other animals. Fishes belong in open waters, so they must be very frustrated and bored when kept in bowls and tanks. If we stop buying fishes, people will stop catching them and selling them.
- If you already have a tank, make sure it's kept at the proper temperature (78° to 82° F for fresh water and 76° to 78° F for salt), is kept somewhere safe but where the fishes can look out, and has a rock garden and aquatic plants for fishes to hide in.
- Don't eat fishes. Just because they look strange doesn't mean they don't count. And, anyway, because of water pollution, fish flesh can be full of mercury and other chemicals that cause human cancers, as well as other contaminated junk that isn't good for us.

CHECK IT OUT

- Write to the **Campaign for the Abolition of Angling,** P.O. Box 14, Romsey, S051 9NN, England, for more ideas on how you can help end sport fishing. Since this group is overseas, be sure to put 44 cents' worth of stamps on your letter to cover postage costs.
- Write to **PETA,** P.O. Box 42516, Washington, DC 20015, for a free fact sheet about fishing.

18 ART IMPACT

Question: Do you like art on a wall?
Answer: I dunno, wouldn't he look kinda strange up there?

DID YOU KNOW?

- On a wall bordering Ocean Park Boulevard in Santa Monica, California, Robert Wyland has painted a beautiful mural of a mother gray whale with her calf and some dolphins swimming free in a turquoise sea. It attracts everyone's attention as they drive or walk by. Your class could do a mural that would get just as much attention as this famous one!
- A mural on a wall or a piece of canvas is an exciting way to call people's attention to animal rights.
- A mural will last for years.
- A wall mural could become a landmark. A canvas mural can be displayed at school, at a fair, at a shopping center, at a bank, and many other places.

WHAT YOU CAN DO

● Ask your art teacher, camp counselor, or club or troop leader if
your class can paint an animal mural.

• A mural could be painted on a school hall wall, in the cafeteria,
on a concrete wall in the neighborhood, or in any suitable place
in or outside of school. Construction companies sometimes welcome murals to brighten up their wooden barricades at construction
sites.
• A canvas mural could be either one huge piece of canvas or
many squares or rectangles of canvas which later could be laced
or sewn together, or attached to one huge piece of canvas backing,
to form the completed project.

● Have each class make one or several sections of the mural or
canvas.

• Students could make pictures on paper and then decide which
picture or pictures they want to use.
• If you want people to work on smaller sections of one big picture
or message, you can divide the picture you like into squares on a
grid, give each person or group one of the squares, and have them
make it to scale.
• PETA has a free coloring poster by Paula de Marta, which could
be used as a mural design. It has instructions on the back for
graphing it out to fit the dimensions of the wall. Write to PETA
kids to get one for your class.

● Some theme suggestions are:

• a modern Garden of Eden, with people and animals living in
harmony. (Don't forget the chickens, cows, pigs, and turkeys!)
• companion animals being treated well by their guardians; add a
message telling the importance of protecting animals.
• an underwater scene at a coral reef or a partly underwater scene
at the edge of a lake.

• a scene with forest animals, saying something like "The original owners of fur coats thank you for not wearing their skins."

• animals leaving their circus cages and returning to the jungle, with a caption like "Animals belong in their natural homes, not in cages."

• a tree with branches filled with birds of all sizes and colors and birds flying in the air around the tree. In a lower corner could be an empty bird cage with a large "X" through it.

CHECK IT OUT

● Check with an art supply store about the materials you need. Select "environmentally friendly" materials when possible.

● Write to many different animal protection groups for a variety of information and pictures on all the themes mentioned to help you with ideas for your artwork.

● Check your school and public libraries for pictures and information.

19 HELP TURTLES OUT OF TROUBLE

Sea turtles live in the water, but sometimes they come up on the beach. Guess why sea turtles go to the beach?

A. To get a tan.
B. To lay eggs.
C. To build a sand castle.

Letter B is correct. Turtles use their back flippers to dig a hole, lay their eggs in the hole, and then cover them up again—all without looking!

DID YOU KNOW?

- Sea turtles have been on the Earth for one hundred million years and live to be more than one hundred years old!
- Sea turtles live in the water but breathe air. When sleeping, they can stay deep in the water for hours without going to the surface

for air. When awake during the day, they have to swim to the top every few minutes to take a deep breath.

- Sea turtles lay up to one hundred eggs at a time. When the baby turtles hatch, they start running for the ocean, which they know is there by the reflection of the moon on the water's surface. Turtles return to the place they were born when they're ready to have babies of their own.

- Other kinds of turtles live on land. Box turtles are the only ones who can completely disappear into their shells, which protect them from all other animals—except people.

- Box turtles often have to cross streets to get to good nesting sites. In places where there are curbs, the turtles often end up falling over onto their backs trying to step up onto the curb—stuck until someone turns them right-side up. Some turtles keep walking along the curb looking for a low spot and get sick from the hot pavement in the summer. Some cities like Minneiska, Minnesota, and Tybee Island, Georgia, have put up warning signs for people in cars to be careful not to run over turtles who cross the street. Some neighborhoods on Long Island, New York, are thinking about lowering their curbs for the turtles.

- The desert tortoise is in danger of becoming extinct. As you can probably guess, these tortoises live where there are few trees but lots of low shrubs to eat and hide under. But ranchers rent land from the government for their cattle to graze. The cattle eat all the shrubs, roots and all, and leave the turtles nothing to eat and nowhere to sleep.

- All-terrain vehicles (ATVs), three- and four-wheel motorbikes, are not only dangerous for people, but also cause problems for tortoises and turtles. People often run turtles over, and their bike paths tear up the turtles' homes.

- Snapping turtles have tails as long as their bodies, and they will chomp in your direction if you try to pick them up. They aren't mean; they're just afraid of people.

WHAT YOU CAN DO

- If you find turtles in a safe place, leave them alone or you'll give them shell shock! Turtles have things to do and places to go. If

you find turtles in a place that isn't safe, let them go in the woods
or in a park nearby. Turtles shouldn't be "pets"; they would rather
live free with other turtles and have their own families.

- If you already have a turtle (one that you or somebody else found)
  at home or school, contact a local wildlife rehabilitator. (Ask your
  local shelter or humane society for names and phone numbers.)
  Wildlife rehabilitators can help turtles who have been kept as
  companions get used to living free again.

- If you have a turtle from a pet store or some other captive situation,
  contact the **Reptile Defense Fund** at 5025 Tulane Dr., Baton
  Rouge, LA 70808. The RDF can give you advice about how to
  get the turtle to a proper sanctuary or refuge. If the turtle isn't
  native to your area, he or she may need to be sent to a more suitable
  habitat in another part of the country.

- If you see turtles on their backs at the side of the road, carefully
  turn them over and put them well away from traffic. When moving
  turtles out of the road, don't put them in ditches or very rocky
  places; put them on nice flat areas of grass or dirt facing in the
  same direction they were going. Long-tailed turtles might be snapping turtles. They can be safely moved out of the street with a
  long-handled shovel—used *gently,* of course. Be gentle, too, when
  turning them back over onto their stomachs, and place them right-
  side up on a soft grassy spot so you don't hurt them or crack their
  shells!

• If you find injured or sick turtles (if, for example, their shells
are cracked or they're bleeding), take them immediately to a turtle
specialist. Call your local humane society or zoo for the name of
a turtle expert near you.

• One young friend of the turtles sings this song whenever she
helps a turtle out of the road:

> Carry the turtle across the road
> Take the time to help a turtle
> Help a turtle across the road
> Help him with his heavy load.

- Add saving desert turtles to the long list of good reasons for not
  eating beef! The less beef we eat, the fewer cattle there will be to

ruin the turtles' homes and eat all the turtles' food. You can save turtles *and* cows at the same time.

- Discourage people from using ATVs and four-wheel-drive cars and trucks in the desert. If they don't want to tear up their own backyards with these bikes, they should consider how unfair it is for them to tear up the homes of turtles, lizards, birds, and other animals.

- Don't buy real tortoiseshell barrettes, brushes, ornaments, or jewelry. Make sure it's plastic before buying anything that looks like tortoiseshell.

CHECK IT OUT

- Write to the **Sea Turtle Restoration Project,** Earth Island Institute, 300 Broadway, Suite 28, San Francisco, CA 94133, for information on helping sea turtles.

- Send $1 to the **Reptile Defense Fund,** 5025 Tulane Dr., Baton Rouge, LA 70808, for a copy of their brochure called *Ten Things You Can Do to Protect Reptiles and Amphibians.*

20 | STICK IT TO 'EM!

Question: What did the lovesick animal rights sticker say to the handsome notebook binder?
Answer: I'm stuck on you!

DID YOU KNOW?

- One of the best skateboarders around these days, Mike Vallely, is an animal rights activist. People all over the world who go to see his skateboarding skills recognize Mike by his board, which says, "Please don't eat my friends." A company called **SMA World Industries** has even started selling skateboards sporting Mike's kind message!
- With stickers you can add style to those boring notebook binders and at the same time tell your classmates and teachers that you really care about animals.
- You can educate lots of mail carriers with every letter you send. (Read on to find out how.)

- "Wheelie-cool" bikes are those that have animal rights stickers all over them!
- Brighten bumpers with animal rights stickers. Give your parents, brothers, sisters, and friends (anyone who drives) stickers to put on their car so they can use traffic time to tell others on the road that animals have rights and need to be protected.
- Put a button on your jacket, and then you can button your lip and still tell others about animal rights.

WHAT YOU CAN DO

- Order a custom-made rubber stamp with your own message from an office supply store or mail-order service. Use it to decorate envelopes, letters, and other surfaces with animal-friendly phrases like "Stop Animal Testing" or "Vegetarians Eat for Life."
- Plaster animal rights stickers all over your notebook binders, folders, bike, skateboard, and (with permission) the family car(s).
- Call a sign shop and find out how much it would cost to have magnetic backing cut and applied to your bumper stickers. Every day you'll be able to move your stickers to different positions on your car—on the hood, the roof, and on the doors.
- For your locker, glue magnets on the backs of stickers that still have backing, and you won't get in trouble because they won't stick permanently.
- You can order buttons from party supply stores with any animal message you want. Think of mottoes, draw your own pictures, or clip photographs of animals out of magazines. Or make your own if your group or club has a button maker. You can sell buttons to others at your school—or whenever you set up an information table.
- Order stickers, leaflets, and cards about animal testing to have on hand for whenever you see an opportunity to tell others about cruel products.
- Make sure that every menu you open that features meat gets an information card about the cruelty and dangers of eating animals, so that the next person who stops by for a burger learns the facts. (**PETA**'s "Are You Really That Hungry?" cards are perfect!)

CHECK IT OUT

- If you like to skateboard and don't like to eat animals, write to **SMA Industries,** 3848 Del Amo #304, Torrence, CA 90503, for information on how you can order a skateboard like Mike Vallely's.
- Write to **PETA,** P.O. Box 42516, Washington, DC 20015, for a free catalog that includes bumper stickers and buttons telling others "Meat Stinks," "Fur Is Dead," you're a "Caring Consumer," and other animal rights messages. Also ask about cards and envelope stickers.
- Stop in or call any local office supply store and ask about ordering a personalized hand stamp to decorate mail and other surfaces with messages of kindness. If you have trouble locating a store in your area, you can write to **Metro Stamp and Seal Company,** 9425 Georgia Ave., Silver Spring, MD 20910, for details about its hand stamps.
- You can order stamps that have positive messages like "Be Kind to Animals, Don't Eat Them," from **Amberwood,** Route 1, Box 206, Milner, GA 30257. Ask for a free catalog that includes the company's complete selection of hand stamps and other cruelty-free products.
- Write to the **Humane Society of the United States (HSUS),** 2100 L St., N.W., Washington, DC 20037, to order bumper stickers that read "Remember the Elephant . . . Forget Ivory" for $3.25 or "Animals . . . It's Their World, Too" for $3.50.
- Write to the organizations listed in appendix C to find out what stickers and buttons they have for sale.
- To make your own buttons, order a starter kit (includes a hand press and other materials) for $29.95 plus $1.75 for postage and handling from **Badge-A-Minit,** 348 N. 30th Rd., Box 800, LaSalle, IL 61301.

PLAYING FAIR

Question: If Grandma gives a Barbie doll to Tanya and a Nintendo game to Leslie, why is *Susie* so happy?

Answer: Because Susie is a rabbit, and Barbie dolls and Nintendo games (as well as hundreds of other toys) are made by companies that don't hurt rabbits or other animals by testing their toys on them.

But some companies *do* test toys that way. For example, LJN Toys tested the "Gotcha" gun by firing paint pellets into rabbits' eyes. Other cruel toy companies rub paints into the animals' skin or force them to swallow play clay and harmful chemicals. When the tests are over, the animals are killed. These toys are no fun!

There are many ways toys, cosmetics, and household products can be tested *without* using animals, such as by using high-tech computers and mathematical models. Companies can also use materials that are already in use and known to be safe. Think of how many animals could be saved if all toys were tested these cruelty-free ways!

DID YOU KNOW?

- You and your family can help save rabbits, guinea pigs, and other animals in laboratories by buying toys from companies that are cruelty-free, such as **Hasbro, LEGO Systems, Tonka, Nintendo, and Mattel.**
- When people decide not to buy any products from a certain company for a certain reason, they boycott the company. Hasbro, Tonka, and Kenner used to conduct tests on animals, but after thousands of people boycotted them, they stopped.
- Barbie lists "animal rights volunteer" among her interests and has campaigned to stop the clubbing of baby seals, dressed in her *fake* fur jacket.

WHAT YOU CAN DO

- Write to **PETA,** P.O. Box 42516, Washington, DC 20015, for free lists of cruelty-free toy companies. Distribute the lists to your friends and relatives and take them with you when you go shopping.
- Send a protest letter to toy companies that still use animal tests. These companies are:

  - **Fisher-Price,** 636 Girard Ave., East Aurora, NY 14052-1885
  - **Shelcore, Inc.,** 3474 South Clinton Ave., South Plainfield, NJ 07080
  - **Spearhead Industries, Inc.,** 9971 Valley View Rd., Minneapolis, MN 55344

Here's a sample letter to a company still using animal tests:

President
Shelcore, Inc.
3474 S. Clinton Avenue
South Plainfield, NJ 07080

Dear President,

I am eight years old and I love animals. I am writing to let you know that I will not buy or accept your company's toys until you stop testing on animals. I like to play, but I won't play with any of your toys because your tests are no fun for the animals.

My friends and I will only buy toys made by Kenner, Hasbro, and other companies that do not hurt animals in tests.

Sincerely,
Stacey Lynn Dryer

- Cleaning your room couldn't be easier! Check out your toys one afternoon. If there are any that are "cruel," send them back to the manufacturer and write a letter explaining why.
- You might also want to complain to toy stores that sell toys tested on animals. In your letter, you might want to say something like "I am writing to tell you that I will not buy any toys that have been tested on animals. Enclosed is a list of the companies that test their toys that way. I hope you will no longer stock their toys. Instead, please sell toys made by companies that *don't* do animal tests." (Write to **PETA**, P.O. Box 42516, Washington, DC 20015, for free lists.)
- If that doesn't work, get some friends together and organize a protest in front of the store! Our country's history is full of stories about people taking to the streets to change our society for the better. Here's how:

 • Before arranging a protest, call your local police station to make sure it's legal to demonstrate (protest) where you want to be. It is usually best to be outside on the sidewalk, where you can talk to lots of passersby before they make their purchases.
 • Once you've figured out where and when you can have the protest, you'll need to gather some materials, such as a large stack of pamphlets or leaflets to hand out and a big poster that describes what you're protesting. Make signs for protestors to carry or wear that have short, snappy slogans such as "Animal Testing Is No

Game'' and ''Nonviolent Toys, Nonviolent Tests.'' Making and wearing animal costumes, even just ears and noses, is a great way to attract attention.

• Before the demonstration, do your homework. Know enough about the kinds of tests that are done on animals, and the companies that do and don't test, to be able to show people you know what you're talking about. Be able to explain why you're protesting a particular store—maybe it was your favorite shop, but the management ignored your letters, phone calls, and visits to try to convince them to carry more types of cruelty-free toys. And be able to tell people what they can do to help stop toy testing on animals.

• Avoid toys like ''Earl the Dead Cat,'' ''Krushed Kitty,'' ''Kickdog,'' and ''Bad Bug,'' which teach that animals are objects to be hit and abused.
• Look for positive games like:

  • ''Dam Builders,'' in which players are beavers. As they collect branches and food for their winter supply, they meet predators, humans, and Mother Nature.
  • ''Save the Whales,'' in which players work together to save eight great whales from extinction.
  • ''Nectar Collector,'' in which players are bees collecting nectar to fill their honeycombs. Along the way, players learn how honeybees work together.
  • ''Endangered Species,'' in which players travel to help save endangered species.
  • ''Colorful Kingdom,'' in which players, aged four to eight, talk and walk like animals and match them to their appropriate habitats.

CHECK IT OUT

• Write to **PETA** for more information about how you can get involved to end toy testing on animals.
• ''Nectar Collector,'' ''Save the Whales,'' and ''Dam Builders'' are available from **Animal Town,** P.O. Box 2002, Santa Barbara, CA 93210. Write to the company for their wonderful catalog of

games, books, puzzles, and musical recordings, many of which focus on animals and nature.

● "Endangered Species" is made by **Teaching Concepts, Inc.**, P.O. Box 150, Jericho, NY 11753.

● "Colorful Kingdom" is made by **Family Games,** P.O. Box 97, Snowdon, Montreal, Quebec H3X 3T3, Canada. Family Games makes many other games and puzzles that challenge and entertain kids while teaching about the animals and the environment.

22 CALL FOR COMPASSION

OPERATOR: May I help you?
ACTIVIST: I'd like to speak with Annie.
OPERATOR: Annie who?
ACTIVIST: Annie-one who can help me help animals!

Can't get a ride to the next animal rights protest? Let your fingers do the walking! Fur companies, cruel cosmetics companies, and other companies that hurt animals often have "800" phone numbers that you can call for free. These numbers let companies keep in touch with the people who buy their products, and you can call to let companies know that kindness to animals—not greed—is *your* priority.

DID YOU KNOW?

- "800" numbers are paid for by the companies that advertise them, not by you, so you can talk as long as you like. In fact, the longer you talk, the better for the animals. When you have politely stated your opinion to the operator, ask to be transferred to a supervisor. If he or she hangs up, you can call back. Become a member of the "frequent phoner" club.

● Companies including **Gillette** and **L'Oréal** have gotten calls from hundreds of animal rights activists on a single day!

WHAT YOU CAN DO

● The following companies sell or promote fur, not yet realizing that we can make fashion statements without killing animals. If you, your parents, or a friend are on their mailing list, you might want to say something like "Hi. I just got your catalog in the mail and couldn't believe that your company is *still* selling fur coats. Animals are killed for fur in awful ways, and they deserve their lives, just as we do. Please don't send me any more catalogs until your company stops supporting such cruelty."

- **Broadway:** 1-800-626-4800
- **Fur Vault:** 1-800-548-2908
- **Neiman-Marcus:** 1-800-NEIMANS
- **Robinsons:** 1-800-777-8910
- **Saks Fifth Avenue Folio Collection:** 1-800-345-3454
- **Seattle Fur Exchange:** 1-800-445-MINK
- **USA FOXX & FURS:** 1-800-USA-FOXX

● The following companies sell items that help people hunt and trap animals. Let them know that in your opinion these activities are cruel and that killing is not your idea of "wildlife conservation." Try saying something like "Hi. I was sad to learn how painful trapping and hunting are for the animals. If you really need to 'capture' animals, try 'shooting' them with a camera and 'catching' them on film."

- **Ted Nugent's Wild Game Hunting:** 1-800-937-WOLF
- **Arrow Walker:** 1-800-338-7389
- **Duke Traps Company:** 1-800-331-5715

- **Hoosier Trapper Supply, Inc.:** 1-800-423-9526
- **Ludy and Mary Trap Co., Inc.:** 1-800-247-7709
- **Tom Miranda:** 1-800-356-6730
- **Northern Fur and Sport Co.:** 1-800-523-4803
- **The Trapper & Predator Caller:** 1-800-258-0929
- **Trappers' Special Products:** 1-800-TRAPPER

● The companies below still test their products on animals. Let them know you're a caring consumer and won't buy their products until they come out of the Dark Ages. Try something like "Hi. I just found out that your company tests its products on animals. There's no excuse for blinding and poisoning animals. More than three hundred companies don't hurt animals to test their products, so I am boycotting your products until you make the switch, too."

- **Bristol-Myers:** 1-800-468-7746
- **Clairol:** 1-800-223-5800
- **Clorox:** 1-800-292-2200
- **Cosmair** (maker of L'Oréal and Lancôme): 1-800-462-2211
- **Fisher-Price** 1-800-432-5437
- **Johnson and Johnson:** 1-800-526-3967
- **L'Oréal:** 1-800-631-7358
- **Nina Ricci:** 1-800-245-6462
- **Noxell Corporation** (maker of Cover Girl): 1-800-638-6204

● Miscellaneous:

- **Adolf Coors Company:** 1-800-642-6116
- **Coca-Cola:** 1–800-GET-COKE

Tell these two companies to "just say 'whoa' " to the rodeo. For years they've been major sponsors of this "sport," in which the animals are prodded and poked and slammed to the ground. You might say something like "I am upset to hear that your company frequently sponsors rodeos. Have you ever thought about how animals suffer in rodeos? Or how they are sent off to the slaughterhouse when they are injured or worn out? My friends and I will not buy your products until you stop supporting animal abuse."

- **USDA's Meat and Poultry Hotline:** 1-800-535-4555

Ever wonder why farmers use chemicals known to be harmful to our health? Here's your chance to ask (and see if you believe the answer)! Call the hot line (Mon.–Fri. 10 A.M.–4 P.M. eastern standard time) with your complaints and questions about the meat industry. You might ask, "Why does the U.S. government give so much money to flesh farmers when the production of meat does so much harm to the earth, the animals and me?"

• **Charles Rivers Laboratories:** 1-800-LAB-RATS

This company supplies schools and laboratories with animals for dissection and experiments.

• **Carolina Biological Supply Company (CBSC):** 1-800-334-5551

• **Ward's Biology:** 1-800-962-2660

The last two companies listed are the country's two largest suppliers of animals for dissection, and a PETA investigation showed that many of the animals are mishandled and abused before they arrive on classroom laboratory tables. Call these three companies, Charles Rivers Labs, CBSC and Ward's, and tell them something like, "I don't believe rats and other animals are our tools to use and throw away as we like. I'm doing my best to make sure my school doesn't order *anything* (or any*body*) from your company."

CHECK IT OUT

● Please note! Sometimes, when companies begin to get lots of phone calls about their treatment of animals, they change their phone numbers. If this happens to any of the above companies, contact **PETA,** P.O. Box 42516, Washington, DC 20015, for information about how to reach them, or make a free call to an "800" operator at 1-800-555-1212 to ask for the new listing.

● If you want to find out whether any other companies not mentioned here have "800" numbers, ask an "800" operator if there's a listing.

23 | TRY IT, YOU'LL LIKE IT

How would you feel if a cow ate you?
Caught you and bopped you,
And chopped you in two,
Fried you or broiled you or put you in stew,
With carrots, potatoes, and an onion or two?
So sometime at dinner when you're starting to chew,
Put down your steak and ponder this through,

How would you feel if a cow ate you?

—PETE TRAYNOR

Most of us grow up eating animals and not even realizing where meat comes from and how it gets to our plates. When we find out, it's usually a shock.

DID YOU KNOW?

- The average American will eat 21 cows, 1,400 chickens, 12 pigs, and 14 sheep in his or her lifetime!
- Today, most pigs, chickens, and other animals bred, raised, and killed for the dinner table have rotten lives. Although pictures on fast-food packages show them having a great time in the outdoors, they don't live that way anymore. Instead, they are most often raised inside crowded sheds, usually unable to turn around because there is so little room. Their offspring are taken away from them almost as soon as they are born, frequently never allowed to play, stretch, or feel the sunlight.
- Studies have shown that killing animals to eat kills *us*, too! The top diseases in the United States are heart disease, cancer, and stroke—all of them strongly linked to eating meat. Your chances of getting these diseases when you get older are very small if you stop eating animals early in life.
- When land is used to raise animals instead of crops, precious water and soil are lost, trees are cut down to make land for grazing or factory farm sheds, and chemicals are used to fatten up the animals quickly and then end up in streams and in the earth.
- Nowadays, there are tons of vegetarians: people who won't eat animals because they care about animals, their own health, and the environment. Some people are vegans (pronounced VEE-gun): people who don't eat *any* animal products including eggs and dairy products.

   • Leonard Nimoy, *Star Trek*'s Mr. Spock, says he's a vegetarian because "superior species" don't kill to live.
   • Ex-Beatle Paul McCartney, his wife, Linda, and their kids are all "veggie" because they love the lambs and sheep on their farm and would rather see them die of old age than be baked in the oven.
   • Dave Scott, the only athlete ever to win the grueling Ironman Triathlon more than once (he has won it six times!), is a vegetarian—as is world-famous hurdler Edwin Moses.

- J. H. Kellogg, the man who started the Kellogg's cereal company, was a vegetarian. He used to say, "I don't eat anything with a face!"
- Country singer and Grammy Award winner k.d. lang is a vegetarian who feels so strongly about the benefits of not eating meat that she did a TV public service announcement, saying, "We all love animals, but why do we call some 'pets' and others 'dinner'?"
- Other well-known vegetarians include: Louisa May Alcott, Lisa Bonet, Christie Brinkley, Cesar Chavez, Albert Einstein, St. Francis of Assisi, Daryl Hannah, Chrissie Hynde, Michael Jackson, Howard Jones, Tony La Russa, Cloris Leachman, Sabrina Le Beauf, Annie Lennox, Casey Kasem, Madonna, Steve Martin, River Phoenix, Plato, Martha Plimpton, Fred ("Mr.") Rogers, Albert Schweitzer, George Bernard Shaw, Isaac B. Singer, Henry David Thoreau, Tolstoy, and Leonardo Da Vinci.

● You can get all the protein you need from vegetables, soy products, nuts, rice, wheat, potatoes, and beans. Vegetarians save their health while they save animals.

● A lot of people can't digest milk, and drinking it causes all kinds of problems—from runny noses, to ear infections, to bed wetting! Soy milk tastes great and is much better for you than cow's milk. (You can buy soy milk at most health food stores and some supermarkets.) The vanilla and chocolate varieties taste especially good and usually aren't any more fattening than the regular flavor.

● Elephants, giraffes, bulls, elk, rhinoceroses, moose, and gorillas are all vegetarians—more living proof that you can grow big and strong without eating meat!

WHAT YOU CAN DO

● Being a vegetarian costs less than eating meat, makes mealtimes interesting, and shows you care. You can start slowly rather than stop all at once, or you can switch your diet overnight. Here are just some ideas of what to eat instead of pigs, cows, chickens, and lambs:

• Try tofu! It sounds like "toad food," but it's an amazing people food that has been eaten in China for over two thousand years. Now it's here in the United States. Don't try it raw or you'll never try it again. Crumbled tofu can be scrambled with onions, tomatoes, and curry for breakfast. You can put it in the blender with fresh fruit or lemon juice to make a creamy dip. It can be baked in casseroles; breaded and fried; blended and cooked in pies (like pumpkin and coconut cream); mixed with seasonings, made into patties, and fried for tofu "burgers"; and frozen, thawed, sliced, smothered in barbecue sauce, and cooked on the grill to satisfy every barbecue lover's desire. It is full of protein and iron.

• Baked potatoes (including sweet potatoes) are easy to make and fun to eat! If you have a microwave, you can bake a potato in only seven or eight minutes, depending on its size. Then you can put all kinds of good things on it: margarine, Bac*Os (made from vegetables, of course!), ketchup, barbecue sauce, Italian salad dressing, or tofu "sour cream" (half a pound of soft tofu blended at high speed with ¼ cup of oil, 1 tablespoon lemon juice, 1½ teaspoons sugar, and ½ teaspoon salt).

• Use your noodle! Go Italian with great easy-to-make spaghetti. Cook some pasta and pour your favorite (nonmeat) spaghetti sauce over it—presto! Try different shapes, colors, and flavors of noodles. At health food stores and some grocery stores you can find whole-wheat noodles, spinach noodles, noodles made with tomatoes or artichokes, noodles in different shapes and sizes, and even noodles that look like poodles!

• Did you know that broccoli contains more calcium per calorie than any other food? (Move over milk!) Vegetables like broccoli, cauliflower, kale, Brussels sprouts, and spinach taste great even though they're good for you. If you don't like these vegetables straight off the stove top, right out of the microwave, or raw, use your imagination to spice them up! Dill, garlic, curry, onion salt, or Italian salad dressing can add a lot to plain vegetables. Some people like barbecue sauce on their cauliflower, and many people put a little lemon juice on their spinach. Try all kinds of things until you find what you like. Green leafy vegetables are a great source of calcium, iron, and vitamin C.

- After a feel-good veggie meal, spoil yourself with a veggie dessert! Look in the freezer section of your local health food store for **Tofutti**-brand creamy desserts and **Rice Dream,** an ice-cream substitute made from rice! A grocery store chain on the East Coast, **Giant Foods,** even has its own brand of dairy-free dessert, called "Dreamy Tofu."
- Borrow a vegetarian cookbook from the library and throw your burgers to the wind. Try a whole bunch of different recipes until you've found your new favorites.
- Volunteer to cook dinner once a week for your family, and provide them with great veggie meals!
- If your family is not vegan or vegetarian, ask if they're willing to eat vegan one or two nights each week.
- Test your knowledge of international veggie foods. In a movie called *Vegetarianism: A Way of Life,* William Shatner, who played Captain Kirk in *Star Trek,* takes a trip around the world visiting kids and their families. Can you guess what he finds people eating? In Mexico, veggie kids bite into bean b____tos; in China they chomp on chop s____; in Italy tasty tomatoes top sp____i marinara; and American kids preferred p____ b____ and j____ sandwiches!

CHECK IT OUT

- Flip to the end of this book, appendix B, for some tasty, easy recipes you can make by yourself. Try cooking from these recipes for a bake sale fund-raiser, holiday pot luck, or birthday surprise meal for Mom—or just for fun!
- Send $2.50 to the **Vegetarian Resource Group,** P.O. Box 1463, Baltimore, MD 21203, for a copy of their book, *I Love Animals and Broccoli.* The book is full of information, puzzles, games, stories, and quizzes for young vegetarians and kids who are thinking about becoming vegetarian.
- Ask for a subscription to *Vegetarian Times* magazine, Box 446, Mount Morris, IL 61054, for your birthday. The monthly magazine is packed with recipes, interviews with celebrities who are vegetarians, and the latest info on how you are affected by what you eat.

- Send $3 to **PETA**, P.O. Box 42516, Washington, DC 20015, for a full-color wall chart for your kitchen. The "Healthy Eating" chart explains which vegetarian foods are high in which vitamins, what tastes good and what doesn't, and lots of other things that will make the switch to vegetarianism easier than saying "Perfect pigs play preciously in plush pastures!"

- While you're at it, include a self-addressed, stamped envelope for a free "Meat Stinks" button or bumper sticker, and ask for a free postcard you can send to a friend to spread the word about vegetarianism. PETA also has lots of free vegetarian recipe cards and tons of information on vegetarianism and factory farming.

- Send £18.50 (that's British pounds, approximately $28) for the twenty-minute video on vegetarianism, *Food Without Fear,* produced by The Vegetarian Society of the U.K. Be sure to ask for VHS tape in U.S. format ("NTSC"). Write to **The Vegetarian Society,** Parkdale, Dunham Rd., Altrincham, Cheshire WA14 4QG, England. Maybe your group can buy it—and pass it on to others when you've seen it. Your library may also be interested in buying a copy. Anyone can borrow a copy from PETA for a month—just send a $15 deposit (refunded when you return the tape).

- Become a member of Compassion in World Farming's **Farm Animal Rangers,** 20 Lavant St., Petersfield, Hampshire GU32 3EW, England. For £2 (that's British pounds, roughly $3.50) you'll receive a folder with buttons, stickers, and information; a subscription to their kid's magazine, *OUT;* and information on their pen pal program, Pen Pal Link-up.

24 | CHECK OUT THE ENTERTAINMENT!

What do bears like to do?

A. Wear tutus and dance.
B. Pick and eat wild berries.
C. Teeter on tightropes.

The answer is B. They find the others un*bear*able!

DID YOU KNOW?

- Some circuses travel twelve thousand miles every year. You would have to drive across the United States (from San Francisco to Washington, D.C.) four times even to come close to the number of miles many circus animals travel. You know how boring long trips are, so imagine how the animals feel, cooped up in hot cages!
- Many animals who are used in circuses, like tigers, bears, and alligators, have their teeth and claws removed so they can't strike back.

● Animal performers often learn their tricks by being prodded or beaten. Because they are afraid of being hurt, they perform stupid and sometimes dangerous tricks. Elephants don't normally do headstands. If you weighed a whopping four to five tons, you probably wouldn't want to do one either!

WHAT YOU CAN DO

● People who go to the circus often forget about the animals behind the costumes and bright lights. If you see performing animals, use this checklist to check off the problems you see:

• Are the animals wearing chains and muzzles? Are they wearing silly costumes?
• Does the trainer hold a whip?
• Do the animals have sores, cuts, or scars?
• Are animals forced to jump through flaming hoops? (Animals are afraid of fire.)
• Do they look happy or sad?
• How many unnatural and dangerous stunts do the animals perform, such as riding bicycles, skating, "dancing," walking upright, and balancing on balls?

● Send your checklist to the local paper with a letter asking others to boycott the event. Or ask your teacher to have a discussion group or let you write a paper about what you've seen.
● Imagine yourself in their shoes (or roller skates!). Think of something you don't like to do, like mowing the lawn or giving speeches in front of your class. What if you had to do it *twice* every day? How would you feel if you were kept in a small cage when you weren't performing? It's easy to understand why animal performers look sad and lonely.
● When the circus comes to your town, write a letter to the editor of your newspaper. Your letter will give many people a peep behind the scenes. Let people know that while kids may dream of running away *to* the circus, animals must dream of running *from* it. Your letter might look something like this:

Editor
Times Picayune
555 Main Street
Ourtown, MO

Dear Editor:

Recent advertisements for the circus have bothered me very much. I told my parents I do not want to see the circus this year because now I know that circus animals have a very hard life. They spend many of their days traveling with little food or water in uncomfortable train cars. During training, they may be whipped or beaten. Bears have even had their noses broken. It makes me sad to see elephants standing on their heads or tigers jumping through rings of fire because I think they would rather be running through the jungle or sleeping in the grass. My family and I will not be going to the circus, and I would like others to consider not going either.

Sincerely,
[Your name]

- Get a group together to protest outside the circus. You can dress up as clowns or wear animal costumes or masks and hand out information. If you know people who can juggle or ride a unicycle, bring them with you. Like the dog who went to the flea circus and stole the show, you may, too! Many people aren't aware that animals may not be having as much fun as they are; let them know better.

CHECK IT OUT

- Round up your family and friends to see the **Cirque du Soleil** (Circus of the Sun), the **Pickle Family Circus,** or the **Circus Oz.** Fabulously entertaining, these circuses use only human performers.
- Write to **PETA,** P.O. Box 42516, Washington, DC 20015, for a free circus leaflet, fact sheet, and poster. Copy the leaflets and fact

sheets to hand out at the circus, and use the poster at your demonstration.

● Pat Derby, a former animal trainer, left the spotlight and now helps animals used in entertainment. She formed the **Performing Animal Welfare Society (PAWS),** an organization devoted to helping animals used in circuses, films, and television get humane treatment. Write to **PAWS, P.O.** Box 842, Galt, CA 95632, for more information on how you can help performing animals.

● Send a self-addressed, stamped envelope to the **Progressive Animal Welfare Society** (also called **PAWS**), 15305 44th Ave. West, P.O. Box 1037, Lynnwood, WA 98046, and ask for "The Bear Friends Coloring Book," an eight-page story about kids who realize circuses are only fun for people.

25 DRESS TO A "T"

Question: Who designs the coolest jeans?
Answer: You! Equipped with paint, patches, colorful stitches, and positive be-kind-to-animals messages, your jeans will be truly one of a kind. Remember, compassion is the fashion.

DID YOU KNOW?

- You can wear your heart on your sleeve (or on your knees, or on your back, or anywhere) as you spread animal rights messages without saying a word.
- Jazz up your jeans and your jacket! Put a raccoon patch on your coat that tells others, "Save Our Skins." Embroider your jeans with animals and mottoes like "Love Animals, Don't Eat Them" and "Rats Have Rights!"
- You can do it yourself; it doesn't cost much to custom-make your own designer T-shirts, jeans, or jackets!

WHAT YOU CAN DO

● For your animal rights T-shirts, you'll need to get the following:

• Plain all-cotton T-shirts. You can find them at almost any drugstore or department store, and the shirts are sometimes cheaper in packs of three.

• Fabric ("textile") paints or waterproof fabric markers, which you can find at school or buy at art supply stores or fabric shops. Use paintbrushes, or get up to your elbows in paint and use your hands!

• A wide piece of cardboard. If you don't have any at home, ask at a grocery store for a cardboard box.

● Once you have the materials listed above, think of what you would like your T-shirt to show or say. You might want to try it on paper first so you'll have a good idea of what your design will look like before you put it on the shirt. Then you're ready to start.

● To make sure there are no wrinkles, "dress" the wide piece of cardboard with the T-shirt stretched out over it. By putting the piece of cardboard into the T-shirt, you can be sure that the colors will not seep through the fabric to stain the other side. It will also protect the surface you are working on

● Be creative! You can paint, embroider, or design a patch with anything—a picture, a poem, or simply a kind message. Use your imagination!

CHECK IT OUT

● Look through books and magazines about animals to get ideas for designs to paint on your T-shirt.

● Look at the pamphlets, magazines, bumper stickers, buttons, and posters of various animal protection organizations for mottoes and messages.

Question: What did the half note say to the sixteenth note when he sang off key?
Answer: Uh-oh . . . you're in treble now!

DID YOU KNOW?

- Everyone's musical. We all have drums in our ears!
- Not all cowboys rope calves, ride bulls, and say "yessiree!" when offered spare ribs. Some stay home from rodeos so that they can sing songs about animal rights. Here's part of a song by some tunesters from North Carolina:

> I'm just a vegetarian cowboy,
> Perhaps that might sound strange.
> A vegetarian cowboy,
> Right home on the range.

So, don't call me a turkey,
And please don't have a cow.
I'm just a vegetarian cowboy—
Right here, right now!

My boots aren't made of leather,
My jacket isn't of suede,
This cotton belt I'm wearin,
And I'll never ever trade.
—"SOUTHERN WINGS"
(written by Vickie and Scott Beck)

- Lots of musicians incorporate animal sounds into their music, and some have made popular albums of this interspecies music. You can also buy recordings of animal sounds, such as whales' songs and the sounds of birds and insects.
- Some animal protection and environmental organizations have made record albums that feature popular musicians singing about animal abuse and our planet's fragile condition.
- Whether it's rock, jazz, or country, almost everyone likes and listens to music, and radio stations can reach millions of listeners.

WHAT YOU CAN DO

- Ask your teacher to play records of animal sounds in class. Students could write an essay about how the sounds make them feel or what the sounds mean, or they could draw pictures relating to them.
- Write your own songs about animals and the importance of protecting them.
- Substitute words for commercials that use jingles or music to promote animal products. Think of commercials that use songs to advertise fast-food restaurants, hot dogs, and products tested on animals, and change the words to describe how animals are used to create the products. Here are a couple sent to us by a PETA Kid:

• Oh, I'm glad I'm not an Oscar Mayer wiener
That is what I'd truly hate to be
'Cause if I were an Oscar Mayer wiener
I would surely be a dead piggy

• Get a little closer
Careful what you buy
Mice aren't treated nicely
To test Arrid Extra-Dry

● Call local radio stations to request animal rights songs. If the station doesn't have the albums *Tame Yourself* (on Rhino Records), *Animal Liberation* (WAX TRAX!), or *Rainbow Warriors* (Geffen Records), tell the disk jockey that you'd like to hear tunes from these three fabulous albums in the future.

● If your favorite singers or bands haven't yet taken up animal rights issues, write to them in care of their record labels and encourage them to get involved. Send them information and names and addresses of animal rights organizations.

● Take a deep breath and hit the stage. Sign up for your school's talent show and sing your own song, or do a rap, about animals.

● Use animal-friendly music to practice an instrument (including your voice) or in music lessons or class.

CHECK IT OUT

● Look for records by Paul Winter in your library or music store. He uses the sounds of nature and animals in his music. Some of his recordings are *Wolf Eyes, Whales Alive,* and *Voices of the Planet.*

● Look for recordings by other musicians who use animal songs:

• Order an album of music by people with turkeys, wolves, orca whales, and others, for $11.25 from **Interspecies Communication,** 273 Hidden Meadow Lane, Friday Harbor, WA 98250.

• **The Nature Company** has cassette tapes and compact discs such as *Gorillas, Morning Songbirds,* and *Summer's Evening.* You can call 1-800-227-1114 for more information.

• **The Ecology House** stores (located at 341 S.W. Morrison, Portland, OR 97204, 503-223-4883; 1441 Pearl St., Boulder, CO 80302, 303-444-7023; and 49 Exchange St., Portland, ME 04101, 207-775-1281) have a wide selection of tapes, too.

● Order the tape *We're All in This Together: 15 Ecology Songs for the Whole Family,* put together by singer-songwriter Nancy Schimmel and singer/musician Candy Forest with the Singing Rainbows Youth Ensemble, ages nine to fifteen, and other talented musicians. Send $11 (postage paid) to **Sisters' Choice Recordings and Books,** 1450 Sixth St., Berkeley, CA 94710, for this wonderful collection of folk, rock, and jazz songs about pet overpopulation, animals used for tests and dissection, endangered species, the disappearing rain forest, and other related issues. Songs include "Fix My Dog," "Eating Up the Forest," "Who's Gonna Save the Ark," "Just Like We Do," and "Fancy Face Waltz" (music and lyrics on pages 103–104).

• If you're interested in keeping up with the group and sharing your creative projects (songs, poems, and stories about animals and the environment) with them, become a member of the **Association of Rainbow Kids** (**ARK**) (send your letter to Sister's Choice, address above). You'll receive a full-color poster, membership card, and newsletters that *you* can contribute to!

● Order a tape of fourteen animal songs for young children called *Oh, the Animals* by singer-songwriter David Williams. Send $11 to **Trapdoor Records,** P.O. Box 5584, Springfield, IL 62705. *Oh, the Animals* includes songs about the dolphins who don't want to get caught in tuna nets, whales in the ocean, and a little pig who doesn't like ham and bacon.

● Send $1 for a copy of *Otterwise*'s special Winter 1990/1991 "Music Issue" to **Otterwise,** P.O. Box 1374, Portland, ME 04104.

● Try making your own cassette recording of animals "talking," like dogs barking, cats meowing, and birds and people singing.

● Get in touch with the **National Society of Musicians for Animals** (**NMSA**), P.O. Box 436, Redding Ridge, CT 06876, for information about songbooks and tapes. You can order their tape, *Let the Animals Live* for a special kids' price of $8.

● Put together your own mini–music library of animal-friendly recordings. Check your local record store for:

• *Tame Yourself,* which features songs by the B-52's, Belinda
Carlisle, Jane Wiedlin, Howard Jones, Erasure with Lene Lovich,
Aleka's Attic, and others. You can order the cassette from PETA
for $8 or the compact disk for $12 (both include postage). With
your order, you'll also become the newest member of PETA Kids
(if you're not one already). Write to Tamed Musikids, c/o **PETA
Kids,** P.O. Box 42516, Washington, DC 20015.
• *Rainbow Warrior,* a collection of songs that features U2, Sting,
R.E.M., Talking Heads, INXS, Peter Gabriel, and other artists.
You can order it for $7.99 from **Greenpeace,** 1611 Connecticut
Ave., N.W., Washington, DC 20016.
• PETA's first record, *Animal Liberation,* with songs by Howard
Jones, Lene Lovich and Nina Hagen, Captain Sensible, Attrition,
Chris and Cosey, Shriekback, and others. You can order the album
for $7 or the compact disk for $12. You'll also receive a year's
membership to PETA Kids (if you're not already a member). Write
to Liberated Musikids, c/o **PETA Kids,** P.O. Box 42516, Wash-
ington, DC 20015 (offer good while supplies last).

● Ask your music class to perform Jane Wiedlin's hit song ''Fur''
and the Singing Rainbows' song ''Fancy Face Waltz'' (sheet music
for both on following pages). Talk to your piano or voice teacher
about including them in performances. Others will see that you
mean what you sing!

FUR

words & music: GARDNER COLE and JANE WIEDLIN

3rd VERSE:

we've all got a brain
so let's use it
fur means pain
and plenty of abusing

tell your mama tell your aunt
tell everyone you see
fur coats on people are history

INGRID NEWKIRK

The SINGING RAINBOWS YOUTH ENSEMBLE

Fancy Face Waltz

Country Waltz

Words by Nancy Schimmel
Music by Candy Forest

2. To make sure that it's safe,
   they try the make-up in a bunny's eyes.
   They don't want us to know
   because it hurts, as you'd expect.
   There's other tests that they can do.
   so I make sure and so will you,
   that our make-up's not just fun to use,
   it's double-checked. So that it's . . .

3. It isn't just the fancy stuff
   that makes a bunny's life so tough.
   It's toothpaste and detergent,
   it's cleanser and shampoo.
   But when your hair and face are clean,
   it needn't mean that you are mean.
   'Cause you can use the kind
   that lets the love shine through.
   The kind that's . . .

27 | BE AN ELEFRIEND: GET THE ELEFACTS

"Elephant Rap"

Yo everybody we're here to say
Don't buy ivory or you're gonna pay.
The elephants are dying in a major way,
So stop buying ivory—today.

The elephants are dying. Don't you understand?
They need their tusks, and lots more land.
Don't get mad if you don't agree,
Just stop buying ivory.

So now you know they're really in trouble.
So spread the word—on the double.

Whatever you do, don't say you can't.
We really got to save the elephant.

—SHIN INOUYE, DENNIS DAY, AND NICOLE GALLO
Mr. Jacob's sixth-grade class,
Wheeler Avenue Elementary School
Valley Stream, N.Y. 1990

Reprinted from *The Comeback Trail*
Defenders of Wildlife

DID YOU KNOW?

- Elephants can live to be seventy years old in their natural homes, but because of the ivory trade, fewer and fewer older elephants are found in Africa and Asia, where their homelands are.
- Elephants have six sets of teeth during their life, while humans only have two. They have five nails on their front feet and four on their back feet; they walk on the tips of their toes.
- Elephants are good swimmers and can use their trunks like snorkels.
- Elephant herds have a leader—usually the oldest and largest female. Baby elephants stay with their families for their entire lives and are raised by their mothers, aunts, and sometimes older sisters. Members of the elephant family look out for one another.
- In 1988, a herd of elephants brought one of their babies to a park ranger's office for help. When the baby was hurt, the entire herd walked the two miles to the ranger's office where the baby could recover, safe from other animals in the forest.
- An elephant named Siri was found drawing with a rock (held by her trunk) on the floor of her small cell at a zoo! Her keeper watched her draw beautiful designs, stopping to feel the designs with the tip of her trunk every once in a while until she decided the pictures were complete. He was so thrilled that he gave Siri some paper and a charcoal pencil for her to draw with; and Siri was happy to have something creative to do with her time in the zoo. Her drawings can be seen and her story read in the book *To Whom It May Concern* by David Gucwa and James Ehmann. Although it was

written mostly for adults, kids can read it, too. Ask for it at your library or bookstore.

● When poachers kill the adult elephants in a family for their tusks, they have little reason to kill the tuskless babies. Instead, the hunters tie up the young elephants, beat them until they stop fighting back (often called "breaking" an animal), and sell them to circuses, zoos, theme parks, and individuals to keep for amusement or profit.

WHAT YOU CAN DO

● Don't buy or accept anything made of ivory or elephant skin.

  • Although bringing ivory into this country is now against the law, a lot of it is still around from before the ban on ivory. Tell stores that sell ivory that you don't want a piece of dead elephant.
  • Before buying anything that looks like ivory, be sure it's plastic! Fake ivory is now popular to make piano keys (they used to be made of the real stuff) and is carved into ornaments, shaving brushes, and hairbrushes.
  • If you get a gift made of ivory, tell your gift giver that you appreciate the thought, but could they please exchange it for something else. Be sure to explain why.

● Students at Valley Stream Elementary Schools, District 24, New York, built a four-foot-tall papier-mâché elephant that they wheel through the cafeteria during lunchtime. Calling the program "Go Nuts for Elephants," students pay for a chance to guess how many peanuts are in a jar, and they win toy elephants for the closest guess. They send the money they collect to their favorite group working to save the elephants. In what ways can *you* inform your friends and classmates about the dangers faced by elephants?

● Don't visit zoos, circuses, and other places that keep elephants in captivity, and never ride an elephant. Elephants should be free, roaming land in Africa or Asia that is protected from hunters.

- Write to your congressperson and ask him or her to give money
  to the people and organizations that are fighting poachers in Africa
  and Asia. Send your letter to the **U.S. House of Representatives,**
  Washington, DC 20510. Here's a sample letter:

The Honorable [full name]
U.S. House of Representatives
Washington, DC 20510

Dear Representative [last name]:

I am writing to let you know that I am very concerned about
elephants being killed for their ivory. Elephant populations in
Africa are decreasing very quickly, and I am afraid that by
the time I'm old enough to vote, there may not be any elephants left to save. The ways they are killed are very cruel,
and their bodies are left to rot. I hope you will vote for more
tax money to be used to prevent elephant hunting so that the
animals can live freely and the countries where they live can
earn money from tourism. Thank you for remembering the
elephants.

Sincerely,
[your name]

CHECK IT OUT

- Become a Junior Elefriend by sending £6 (that's British pounds,
  about $9: see appendix B) to **ELEFRIENDS,** Cherry Tree Cottage,
  Coldharbour Lane, Dorking, Surrey RH5 6HA, England. You'll
  receive a "Trumpet Elephant Pack," which includes the *Trumpet*
  newsletter, an ELEFRIENDS button, an ELEFACTS poster, and
  a "Babar Says 'Help ELEFRIENDS Help the Elephants' " sticker,
  plus information about how you can help the elephants.

- Write to the **African Wildlife Foundation,** 1717 Massachusetts Ave., N.W., Washington, DC 20036, or call them toll-free at 1-800-344-TUSK, for more information about elephants and what you can do to help.

28 MAKE A MINI–NATURE PRESERVE

Small creature, near me have no fear;
I wouldn't do you harm.
Small lizard, I'm just passing by;
You've no cause for alarm.

Another glance; he sees his chance
To scurry toward the shade
Where none can trifle with his life
And he won't be afraid.

—IDA RIMAN PERCOCO,
Small Wonder

Two caterpillars were lying in the sun when a butterfly flew overhead. Said one caterpillar to the other, "You'll never catch *me* going up in one of those things!"

DID YOU KNOW?

- One tree can be home to over forty animals!
- Where there were once open fields full of blossoms and bushes, and forests full of shady trees, there are now housing developments and shopping centers. Many animals lose their homes when people start building. Luckily, some animals have learned to survive. Birds, squirrels, mice, and thousands of insects live in and around our backyards, and there are many ways you can help them find food and shelter to help them survive in the last remaining spaces.

WHAT YOU CAN DO

- Make your backyard a safe place for small animals. Keep your cat indoors unless he or she is on a leash and harness and you are there to supervise (get a harness made especially for cats at your local companion animal supply store). Put bells on your dogs' and cats' collars so wild animals will hear them coming.
- Plant a berry bush in your yard for the birds and other free-roaming animals to feed from. Snowberries, cranberries, and blueberries are some favorites. Keep some high grasses, too.
- You can buy a birdbath or put water in a pie pan for the animals. The water shouldn't be more than two inches deep because birds and other small animals who fall into deeper bowls of water have a hard time getting out. Be sure to clean out the pie pan every day and fill it with fresh water. Break ice on puddles in the winter so that animals can get a drink.
- Put some dead wood, like old tree stumps and branches, in your yard. More than 150 species of birds and other animals can live in dead trees and logs and feed off the insects there. Never carelessly turn over logs—you will disturb a whole universe.
- Nest-building birds might like some of the soft hair you get from combing your dog, so put it out under the trees and give baby birds a mattress.

- Ask your parents to leave a good part of your yard natural. (Tell them they'll save money on landscaping, lawn mowing and watering as well as help the animals.) Lots of lush trees and bushes, tall grasses that are allowed to go to seed, and even weeds can be used as food and shelter for small animals.
- If you don't have lots of trees or bushes in your yard, start planting. You can send away for a sample tree planting kit for $1 (from **Project Trees for Life,** 1103 Jefferson, Wichita, KS 67203). Visit your local plant nursery to talk to the experts about other plants that help animals.
- When you go hiking, take nothing but pictures and leave nothing but footprints. Stop a few times and just *listen*; hear birds chirping or cawing to one another or small mammals scurrying through the brush. Watch for birds and squirrels in the trees or chipmunks and toads on the ground. Think of all the places in which animals live: nests, trees and logs, holes in the ground, and under rocks.
- Hope Buyukmihci suggests this easy imagination exercise to help us realize exactly how precious each patch of ground is to other-than-humans:

  - Close your eyes and picture the nearest wooded area to where you live. Then, pick a ground-dwelling animal you admire— maybe a squirrel, or a cricket, or a mouse.
  - Now, in your mind, become that animal and make a home for your family with your bare hands, with no tools or help of any kind. Then look for a water source and for food to feed them, just from what you see around. Could you survive in winter or in a dry spell? For how long?

- You can help the bats living outside by buying a bat house from a hardware store or a store that carries wild bird food (look in your telephone book under "Wildlife"). Bat houses give bats a safe shelter during the day when they sleep. Of course, don't disturb them during their sleep! Watch them during and after sunset, soaring and diving for food. These graceful animals will thrill you with their air acro*bat*ics!

CHECK IT OUT

- Get a copy of *Attracting Backyard Wildlife* by Bill Merilees. If your library doesn't have it, you can order one for $10.95 from **Voyageur Press,** 123 N. Second St., Stillwater, MN 55082. It has lots of tips and diagrams that help you give food, shelter, and water to lots of birds, insects, butterflies, small reptiles, and mammals.

- Write for a free copy of "Recycle for the Birds" from the **National Wildlife Federation,** 8925 Leesburg Pike, Vienna, VA 22184, for ideas on easy-to-make birdhouses. To certify your yard in the National Wildlife Federation Backyard Wildlife Habitat Program, write to 1412 16th St., N.W., Washington, DC 20036.

- For free plans for building a house for robins, bluebirds, or other birds, write to **The Kindness Club,** 65 Brunswick St., Fredericton, New Brunswick E3B 1G5, Canada.

- Look for *A Kid's First Book of Birdwatching.* Complete with cassette, it'll teach you how to spot birds by their looks and songs. It's available in many bookstores, or from **The National Audubon Society,** 801 Pennsylvania Ave., S.E., Washington, DC 20003 ($14.95 plus postage).

29 | WRITE ON!

Question: What's black and white and read all over?
Answer: Your letters, of course!

DID YOU KNOW?

- Some cosmetics companies, such as Revlon, stopped testing on animals because they received so many letters asking them to.
- The television game show *Wheel of Fortune* stopped giving away fur coats as prizes after thousands of viewers protested in writing.
- Hundreds of kids decided to get involved in helping animals after reading a magazine article about movie star River Phoenix and his strong belief in animal protection.
- Many people got upset and wrote to a company whose greeting cards had pictures of animals looking as if they were about to fall or be hurt. These letters made the company realize that people like

to see pictures of happy animals and that putting animals in dangerous situations is no laughing matter!

- The mice in a Maryland school district no longer have to fear sticky glue traps. Thanks to many letter writers, mice who wander into the district's schools looking for food and shelter are now released, unharmed, outside.

WHAT YOU CAN DO

The animals can't speak out for themselves, but you can *write* against the wrongs!

- It's great if you can type your letters, but if you can't, you only need a pen and paper to send your messages of kindness. Make sure you write as neatly as you can—remember, if people can't read your letter, they might throw it away. You might want to write a rough draft first; then, when you're sure of what you want to say, copy the letter onto a new piece of paper.
- You can write for your school newsletter. (If your school doesn't have a paper, talk to a teacher about starting one.) You can devote an entire issue to animal abuse and ways to help stop it. You can use information from animal protection groups to share the facts about animal experimentation, fur, and hunting. Include some easy vegetarian recipes!
- Talk to your teacher(s) about toy and cosmetics companies still using animal tests. Your class can write protest letters. Make sure to include the following:

  • Tell the company that you know there are better ways than cruel product tests to make safe products. After all, lots of companies use alternatives such as human volunteers, natural, known safe ingredients, or even artificial skin (this may sound kind of creepy, but it's not as creepy as using live rats, guinea pigs, and rabbits).
  • Encourage the company to use modern, nonanimal methods. Many cruelty-free companies use computer programs that can tell if an ingredient will harm a person's eyes or skin. There's no excuse for blinding bunnies!

• Let the company know you won't buy its products until it stops using animals (and that you'll tell others to boycott, too).
• Ask for a reply to your letter. If you get a fuzzy response, write again. Since the squeaky wheel gets the grease, be a squeaky wheel. Let the company know you will keep writing until you're happy with their answer!

• You should send a polite letter of complaint to any and all stores that offer animal products, such as fur coats, snakeskin clothing, and rabbits' feet. Let the store know you'll shop elsewhere until it stops selling animal suffering—and that you'll encourage others to do the same.

• Make sure to send your concerned response to any newspaper article about animal abuse. If the paper prints your letter, you'll reach many, many readers.

• If your town is planning events that will include animal suffering (such as a circus that uses animal acts), or if it offers carriage-horse rides, put your pen and paper to work. Write a letter to the newspaper(s) in your area and to your local chamber of commerce (you can get the addresses from the phone book). It's important that others know there are plenty of ways to have fun without harming animals.

• Become an expert on factory farming, animal testing, or any animal protection issue, and earn an "A" at the same time: when it's time to write a report, choose an animal rights topic!

CHECK IT OUT

• Write to your legislators about issues such as cosmetics testing on animals, veal crates, or leg-hold traps. You can call your local League of Women Voters to find the addresses of your legislators.

• Join **PETA Kids,** P.O. Box 42516, Washington, DC 20015. You'll receive a newsletter and the action bulletin *Brainstorm* throughout the year; both are full of information on animal rights issues, including where to send your letters. A one-year membership is $3.

• Write to **PETA** for a free packet of information on vegetarianism, animals in entertainment, or any other animal rights issue. You'll receive lots of material to include in your report. (Remember to ask for it when the assignment is given, *not* the night before it's due!)

● Here's a sample letter to the editor:

Greg Nelson
4124 Kindness Court
Crystal Lake, IL 60367
555-7890

July 12, 1990
To the Editor
The Crystal Daily Banner
P.O. Box 346
Crystal Lake, IL 60367

Dear Editor,

I was sad to read that a balloon launch is to take place at the fair. Balloon launches may be pretty to watch, but the balloons don't just disappear into the clouds. They often end up in the oceans, where sea animals swallow them. Thousands of sea turtles, dolphins, whales, and other creatures die because they thought a floating balloon was food.

I hope that people who are concerned about ocean animals will call the chamber of commerce *today* to protest the balloon launch before it is too late.

Sincerely,
Greg Nelson

30 | BORN FREE, BORED STIFF

FIRST SPIDER MONKEY (reading): It says here I've won an afternoon at the zoo!

SECOND SPIDER MONKEY: What did the loser get?

FIRST SPIDER MONKEY: To spend a *week* there!

DID YOU KNOW?

- Zoos started long ago as menageries, collections of "exotic" wild animals kept by kings and emperors. Then showmen decided the public might pay to see "fierce" tigers, "weird" monkeys, and other "odd" creatures they couldn't find close to home, so city zoos were built. Collectors went to Africa, South America, and Asia to catch animals the public would "ooh" and "aah" over.

- Today, most zoos and marine parks are sad places for animals: simply museums of living beings kept in cement pens and cages or in small pools or outdoor enclosures. Although they get basic food and water, most of the animals don't have much to do and must be going out of their minds with boredom.

- Animals who live where they belong, at home in the jungle, woods, or desert, stay busy building their own dens, nests, or burrows, sniffing the ground and the air for the latest news, and searching for foods they like. They raise their families and stay active in their community.

- Orcas, also known as killer whales, can live to be one hundred years old, but those at marine parks only survive eighteen months to twenty years from the time they're captured.

- Some bottlenose dolphins (who look like Flipper) have developed ulcers because of the stress of being on display. It upsets them to have people staring at them all the time with no place to hide. Since dolphins use sonar to communicate, they become confused when it bounces off the walls of their tiny enclosures. (It must feel a bit like being surrounded by mirrors all the time.)

- Many animals are taken from their faraway homes and shipped in small crates to zoos. It's hard to get animals away from their protective families and friends, so sometimes members of the community or family are killed. For example, mother chimpanzees and older relatives are often shot so collectors can capture their babies.

- When zoos end up with "too many" animals of one species, and when animals grow old, some zoos sell the animals directly (or through dealers and auctions) to people who own "game farms" where people can pay to shoot them.

- Pole Pole (whose name is pronounced "poly poly" and means "slowly slowly") was a baby elephant who was captured to appear in a movie. Her "acting" days ended very quickly, and she was sent to the London Zoo. There she rocked back and forth and banged her head on the bars, trying to escape into a dream world in order not to think about her frustrating life in the concrete prison. She watched as her elephant friends either died or were sent away. Though some people cared enough to fight to improve her life, the plans to finally move Pole Pole to a better park were made too late. After years of sadness, Pole Pole, who was only a teenager of seventeen years, lay down to die, having lost her will to live.

WHAT YOU CAN DO

- Don't go to zoos, aquariums, or marine parks. If people don't go, they won't make any money and will have to close down, which means animals will get to stay in their homes.
- Stay away from dolphin swim programs (just say, "Thanks, but no tanks!"). It may sound like fun to swim with dolphins in a pool, but it can be dangerous to both the dolphins and you. If swim programs become popular, more dolphins will be captured. Dolphins, who are stronger swimmers than humans, have slapped people with their tails and rammed them with their noses. Although the dolphins don't mean to hurt swimmers, they can become frustrated and angry. Plus, dolphins can catch human diseases. Your cold could mean serious health problems for a dolphin.
- If your class is planning a field trip to the zoo, ask your teacher to plan a trip to a museum, park, sanctuary, or cave instead.
- If your teacher or family insists that you go to the zoo, be sure to bring along a pencil and paper to take notes (and a camera, if you can). A girl named Jamie Specht took pictures of the animals she saw at a small zoo, and because she made a complaint, the owners had to improve conditions there. Jamie made a big difference for the animals, and so can you! Peter Batten and the **Animal Welfare Institute (AWI)** suggest that you keep your eyes open for the following:

  • Do the animals have water? Is it clean? Are there shady trees they can lie down under?
  • Do they have company?
  • Can they stand up, lie down, and move around comfortably?
  • How much space do they have to run and roam in? Can they get to private space when they want to escape the stares of the gawking visitors?
  • Do the animals look healthy? Are their coats shiny (a sign of wellness)? Do they have any sores or injuries?
  • Does the area smell? Because of bad zoos and kennels, people sometimes expect animal enclosures to smell, but they shouldn't if the caretakers are doing their jobs.

- Different animals have special needs that should be met. Check to see if the great apes are active. Do they have company and things to do? Or are they in small pens, with nothing to do but eat and sleep? Do the elephants and other large animals have rubbing posts or mounds in their pens? Do the birds have at least two separate perches or roosts? Or can they only fly into walls, fences, or onto the floor if frightened?

CHECK IT OUT

- Because of Pole Pole's sad life, a group called Zoo Check was formed to help inform the public about the problems with zoos. Please write to **Zoo Check,** Cherry Tree Cottage, Coldharbour, Surrey, RH5 6HA, England, for more information. (Don't forget to use an airmail stamp, or use two regular stamps and write "Air Mail" on the envelope.)
- For a more detailed zoo checklist, contact the **Animal Welfare Institute (AWI),** P.O. Box 3650, Washington, DC 20007.
- For lots of information about dolphins and ways to help them, send $2.50 to the **Progressive Animal Welfare Society (PAWS),** P.O. Box 1037, Lynnwood, WA 98046, for their newsletter called *Dolphins in Peril.*
- Contact the **South Carolina Association for Marine Mammal Protection (SCAMMP),** P.O. Box 3233, Myrtle Beach, SC 29578-3233, to learn how to help captive marine mammals.
- Write to **PETA,** P.O. Box 42516, Washington, DC 20015, for free leaflets you can hand out to people outside zoos and aquariums.

31 SAYING GOOD-BYE TO UNINVITED GUESTS

Hurt no living thing:
Ladybird, nor butterfly,
Nor moth with dusty wing,
Nor cricket chirping cheerily,
Nor grasshopper so light of leap,
Nor dancing gnat, nor beetle fat,
Nor harmless worms that creep.
—**CHRISTINA ROSSETTI**

Two cockroaches were munching snacks on top of a garbage pile when one of them began telling his friend about some new people on the block: "I hear their refrigerator is spotless, their floors gleaming, and there is not a speck of dust in the place."

"*Please,*" said the other cockroach, "not while I'm eating!"

Sometimes the tiniest of creatures wanders or flaps into our homes. It is usually a mistake, but mistakes can have a happy ending with a little

122

help from us. Animals need our respect and understanding when they are lost in our houses—frightened and probably wanting very badly to get back outdoors where their homes and families are.

DID YOU KNOW?

- Grasshoppers can jump up to thirty inches at a time. If we were that strong, we could jump a football field in one leap!
- Ants can lift more than fifty times their body weight.
- Squirrels plant trees. They bury so many nuts and seeds during the summer and fall that some of them sprout into trees!
- Bats are the only mammals who fly with wings of skin, not feathers. They use radar to tell how far away an object is, but they see with their eyes.

WHAT YOU CAN DO

Live by the Golden Rule: "Do unto others as you would have them do unto you." When dealing with any lost or confused animals, try to put yourself in their place. Imagine being a frightened little spider, mouse, squirrel, bat, bird, or insect, and help them as you would want to be helped. Remember that they are afraid of people (after all, to them you look as big as a battleship looks to you), and treat them gently and calmly whenever you come across them.

Bats in Your Belfry?

- If bats come into your house, don't be afraid! Bats are very sensitive and gentle animals who do *not* get caught in people's hair! If they get into your home, turn off all the lights and open the doors and windows. They will probably find their own way out. If not, catch them, using a large jar or net. Be very careful not to hurt them. Always wear gloves if you attempt to handle bats, as all animals may bite when afraid.

Bird in Your Bedroom?

- If you find a bird trapped in your house, gently corner him or her in one room. Close off the room from the rest of the house and open the door or the window in the room all the way. Leave the room so the bird feels safe enough to look for a way out. Don't be impatient—as long as the bird isn't hurt, he or she will find the window sooner or later. If the bird has not left by evening, hang a light outside the window and turn off all the lights in the room. He or she will fly toward the outside light. Prevent other birds and bugs from getting caught in your house in the future by keeping screens on your windows.
- Birds can't see glass, and sometimes they fly into windows and hurt themselves.

• If you have a large picture window or sliding glass doors, warn birds not to fly into them by cutting long thin strips of cloth (about one-half-inch wide) and placing them about four inches apart so they hang down in front of the window. (Thanks for this tip go to Carroll Henderson of the **Minnesota Department of Natural Resources,** 500 LaFayette Rd., St. Paul, MN 55155.)

• You can also use the following pattern of a falcon to scare other birds away (you'll need to enlarge it to scale—one square equals one inch), although we hear it's a bit less effective than hanging strips of cloth. Outline the pattern onto a piece of construction or notebook paper and color it black. Then tape the falcon silhouette, in a diving position, near the top of your window.

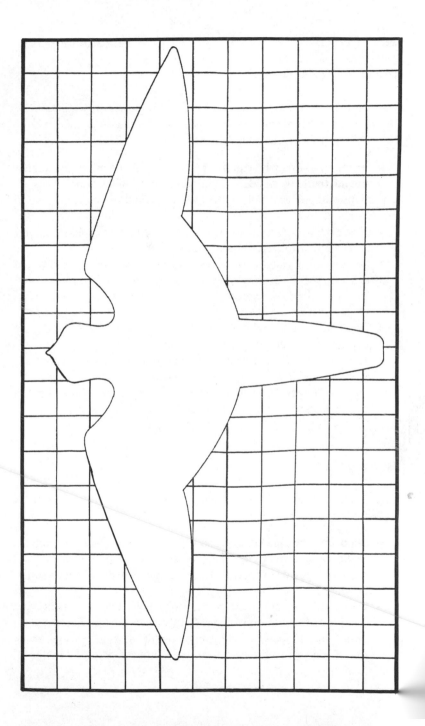

Mouse in Your House?

You can help mice move out by using a live mousetrap, which allows you to release them unharmed outside. When catching mice with a humane trap, follow these guidelines:

- Set the trap somewhere dark where you think the mice are hanging around (perhaps inside a kitchen cabinet where you have seen mouse droppings). Put a little blob of peanut butter in the trap to attract the mice.
- Check the trap every hour. If mice are left in the trap for too long, they get very thirsty and scared.
- Once mice are caught, *rush* them to a field near your house, where there are lots of bushes and plants for them to hide under. If you have more than one mouse, try to take them all to the same place so they can be together.
- Don't catch mice in the winter. They could freeze when suddenly put outside! Wait until spring or summer.
- Always remember that mice and other little animals are very afraid of people and loud noises. When you catch a mouse, be very gentle with the trap and be very quiet around the animal. Place the trap gently on the ground when setting the animal free, and don't make fast, scary movements.

Befriend a Bug

Flies, moths, spiders, and other insects can be helped home with these ideas:

- Keep a bug-release kit handy so you can return these small animals to the outside where they belong. All you need is a see-through glass with a wide opening and a stiff piece of paper or cardboard— period!
- Wait until the insects are resting to put the cup over them, but watch out for legs and wings! Gently slide the cardboard underneath. Just be patient, and eventually you'll get the bugs in the cup. Then you can release them back into the great outdoors.

- Always look in the bathtub before you turn on the shower. It helps to have your clothes on because you may have to run outside with a moth or a spider!

Cockroaches and Ants Get Hungry, Too!

Cockroaches and ants come into our houses for the same reasons mice do—they can't resist food crumbs. In addition to keeping food in sealed containers and wiping up crumbs, you can also try these tricks:

- Wash countertops, cabinets, and floors with a solution of vinegar and water—the same amount of each—to keep ants on the march.
- Place whole bay leaves in several spots around the kitchen (you can find bay leaves with the other herbs and seasonings at the grocery store). Bay leaves smell to cockroaches like old socks do to us, and they'll avoid them. Change them every couple of months or so.
- Pour a line of cream of tartar (ask for it at the grocery store) at the ants' entrance. They won't cross the line!

Don't Do It!

- Never use any kind of sticky glue trap. These traps are very cruel, causing the animals to get their feet, tails, and even their faces stuck in the sticky goo.

CHECK IT OUT

- Ask your parents to get a humane mousetrap from the local hardware store, or order one for $10 from **PETA,** P.O. Box 42516, Washington, DC 20015. They can be used over and over again for years.
- Write to **PETA,** P.O. Box 42516, Washington, DC 20015, for the free fact sheet, "Living in Harmony with Nature."

- Write to **Rat Allies,** P.O. Box 3453, Portland, OR 97208, to find out how you can help improve the image of these unfairly treated animals.
- Contact **Bat Conservation International, Inc.,** P.O. Box 162603, Austin, TX 78716, to learn more about these misunderstood and underappreciated mammals.

32 | TALK TO THE ANIMALS

There was never a king like Solomon
Not since the world began
Yet Solomon talked to a butterfly
As a man would talk to a man
> —RUDYARD KIPLING

A stranger came into a restaurant. At the next table sat a dog and a cat.

As the stranger sat down, the dog rose, yawned, and said, "Well, so long," then walked out.

The stranger's jaw dropped. He said to the waiter, "Did you hear that? The dog talked."

"Don't be a fool," said the bartender. "A dog can't talk."

"But I *heard* him."

"You just *think* you heard him. I tell you dogs can't talk. It's just that wiseguy cat over there. He's a ventriloquist."

Except in cartoons and on TV shows, animals don't usually speak in our language, but they *do* know how to talk in their own way. For several years Professor C. N. Slobodchikoff and his students have been using high-tech equipment to listen to what prairie dogs say in a field in Arizona. They've found that prairie dogs' "voice prints" show different barks in response to the size, shape, and even color of the fur, skin, or clothing of coyotes, snakes, and people going by!

DID YOU KNOW?

- Washoe, one of the family of chimpanzees who has been taught American Sign Language, was raised in a human home. She makes up words such as "water fruit" for watermelon. The first time she bit into a radish she signed, "Hurt cry food." Washoe has taught her adopted chimpanzee son, Loulis, more than seventy of the hundreds of signs she knows.
- When a little kitten bit Koko, an enormous gorilla who knows sign language, Koko signed, "Cat real bad Koko. Teeth visit gorilla!" and gently put the kitten onto the ground. When Washoe first saw another chimpanzee, she was frightened and signed, "Big black bug."
- Talk about making long-distance "caws": Crows in the south of France have a different "accent" from crows in the north!
- Lawrence Kilham, who observed crows for seven years, would often give them corn. On days that he didn't feed them, crows would walk behind him and peck at the bare ground whenever he turned around to let Kilham know they wanted to eat!
- Some believe that dolphins can actually read other dolphins' minds. Their language is made up of "click" sounds—as many as seven hundred a second—and some marine mammal experts believe dolphins can send whole pictures of what they see to other dolphins, just as we see images on a TV screen sent from a station miles away!
- Bees "speak" by dancing. They use different wing flaps to give complicated directions to hive members, allowing them to find flowers miles and miles away!

WHAT YOU CAN DO

If you have a dog or other companion animal, you can practice good communication skills with her or him.

- Are your "conversations" with your dog, cat, or other companions one-sided? When you talk to them, is it only to give commands like "No," "Sit," or "Stay"? Do your animal companions feel as if they are in the army? Give them the time and the freedom to express their feelings. Pay attention to what they say with their eyes, ears, paws, tails, and voices. For example, what are dogs saying when they put their paw on your knee? What do cats mean when they rub against your leg?
- Watch for your companion animals' "body language" and respond to it. Even if you aren't sure what your animal friends are trying to tell you, respond to them. Give them a pat on the head or say, "What is it?" so that they know you aren't ignoring them.
- How many different sounds does your companion make? Can you tell the difference between a happy, excited "I missed you" bark, a "Please let me out" bark, and a bark warning you that someone's at the door? Cats have lots of "voices," too. How many can you recognize?
- Dogs appreciate knowing the rules—it makes their lives easier. But since you speak a foreign language to them, be very gentle and patient, and always use the same word and the same tone for something you want them to learn, or you'll confuse them.

CHECK IT OUT

- Read *Kinship with All Life* by J. Allen Boone (Harper & Row, New York, 1954), a book about a caring man's communications with members of other species.
- Look for Lawrence Kilham's *The American Crow and the Common Raven* (Texas A&M University Press, 1989) in your library or bookstore.

- For tips on how to talk to and train a companion dog, look for a copy of *Mother Knows Best: The Natural Way to Train Your Dog* by Carol Lea Benjamin (Howell Book House, Inc., 1985) or *Communicating with Your Dog: A Humane Approach to Dog Training* by Ted Baer (Barron's Educational Series, 1989).

- To better understand how cats communicate—and how to better communicate with cats—look for *How to Talk to Your Cat: The Guide to a More Fulfilling Relationship with Your Feline* by Jean Craighead George (Warner Books, 1986).

- Order a T-shirt with a design painted by chimpanzee Washoe from **Friends of Washoe,** Central Washington University, Ellensburg, WA 98926.

33 GET YOUR CLASS INTO THE ACT

"You can't fall asleep in my class," said the teacher.
"I could if you didn't talk so loudly," complained the student.

Liven up your class with animals—not in terrariums or cages, or on cutting boards (see chapter 5, "Be Science Fair"), but in books and magazines, through projects and papers, in videos and filmstrips, through actions you take, and in everyone's imagination.

DID YOU KNOW?

- Animals don't belong in the classroom. We can't learn much from captive critters—except that rats, mice, rabbits, guinea pigs, gerbils, hamsters, and turtles get bored and lonely in classrooms!
- It doesn't make sense to use rats in nutrition experiments in class: rats don't make good models for kids. For one thing, rats make their own vitamin C in their bodies, but people have to get it from

their food; and rats need from three and a half to ten times more protein than kids, too.

- In the book *Much Ado About Aldo,* eight-year-old Aldo realizes how unfair it is to keep crickets and chameleons together in a terrarium in his third-grade classroom. Aldo saves the crickets by releasing the chameleons and teaching everyone a lesson in kindness.

WHAT YOU CAN DO

- Ask for a class field trip to a local barn, animal sanctuary, or animal shelter to see how animals are cared for, learn how calves are kept, or find out how you and your class can help injured or stray animals. Kids can write what they think they'll see before they go and afterward write what they *did* see.
- If your class can't go some place special, bring something special to your classroom or auditorium!

• Martita Goshen has a dance program just for kids. Her topics include elephants, the ocean, and Africa, and she travels all over the country to show her love of animals and nature to students through dance. Your teacher(s) can write to Ms. Goshen at **Turtles, Inc.,** 111 Carpenter Ave., Sea Cliff, NY 11579.

• To arrange a singing or storytelling program about treating the world and its inhabitants more thoughtfully, have your teacher(s) contact **Sisters' Choice,** 1450 Sixth St., Berkeley, CA 94710. Nancy Schimmel (storyteller) and Candy Forest (singer) each travel around the country giving performances to kids of all ages and workshops to people age nine and up (even adults!). Ms. Forest often teaches proanimal songs from *We're All in This Together,* a tape she and Ms. Schimmel made with The Singing Rainbow Youth Ensemble, a group of 8 nine- to fifteen-year-olds.

• Singer-songwriter David Williams performs his animal songs, some of which are recorded on a tape called *Oh, The Animals!* for kids all over the country. To invite Mr. Williams to your school, ask your teacher(s) to write to him at **Trapdoor Records,** P.O. Box 5584, Springfield, IL 62705.

• Six members of **Youth for Environmental Sanity** (the YES! Tour) travel all around the country giving presentations, assemblies, and workshops at schools. For more information, ask your principal or a teacher to write them at 706 Frederick St., Santa Cruz, CA 95062.

● Do a class play of *Charlotte's Web,* based on the novel by E. B. White. Students who don't have parts in the play can work on scenery, props, and costumes while the others are rehearsing. (See chapter 41, "Produce a Play.") Maybe you can videotape the performance like a real TV show.

● If animals are kept in your classroom, discuss what your class can do to give them a better life (see chapter 1, "Do Unto Others . . ." for ideas); or, better yet, send them to a *real* home. Talk to your teacher about ways to learn about animals in their natural habitats.

● Start a letter-writing campaign. Pick a topic or case that the class feels strongly about, find out who has the power to change or improve the lives of the animals involved, get that person's address, and start writing! (See chapter 29, "Write On!" for tips on writing letters.)

● Ask one of your teachers to have a class discussion on cosmetics testing, vegetarianism, pet shops, or animals in entertainment.

● When you read stories about animals, notice and discuss what the writer seems to think about animals. Refer to the list in chapter 43, "Be a Bookworm," for positive books about animals.

● Have your class do what Dr. Janice Clarke's African classes have done: make a poacher's cage out of sticks and leaves, then take turns sitting inside it and describing your journey and your feelings, as if you were the unlucky chimpanzee.

● When choosing subjects for school reports, suggest people choose animals many people misunderstand, like rats, snakes, spiders, bats, wolves, or octopuses. Make yourselves the local experts on these types of animals. Make one species your theme for projects and sing its praises through your art and words.

CHECK IT OUT

● Get competitive! Have the whole class enter a contest for the animals.

• Every year, the **New England Anti-Vivisection Society** has a Creative Arts Competition for students in grades six and up. Students express their concepts of animal rights in any of three areas: literary arts (poetry, short stories, plays, and the like); fine arts (painting, sculpture, drawing); and audiovisual arts (photography, film, video or sound recordings). There are cash scholarships for each age group (grades six through eight, grades nine through twelve, and college) and a grand prize of $1,000. Entries are usually due at the beginning of June. For more information write to NEAVS, 333 Washington St., Suite 850, Boston, MA 02108.

• **The Kindness Club** has an annual essay contest for U.S. and Canadian kids in grades five to eight. There are prizes for the top entries, and essays are due each year in November. For topics, write to The Kindness Club Essay Contest, 65 Brunswick St., Fredericton, New Brunswick, E3B 1G5, Canada.

• The **Vegetarian Resource Group** also has an annual essay contest for students, with a first prize worth $50. For more information, write to the Vegetarian Resource Group, P.O. Box 1463, Baltimore, MD 21203.

● Ask each person in your class to contribute fifty cents toward a class membership in an animal protection group (see appendix B for ideas). Or have a fund-raiser such as a vegan bake sale or a car wash to cover the membership cost.

• A $20 subscription with the **National Association for Humane and Environmental Education** entitles a class to thirty-two copies of each bimonthly issue of *Kind News Junior* (grades two to four) or *Kind News Senior* (grades five to six). Write to NAHEE, 67 Salem Rd., East Haddam, CT 06423, about subscriptions to *Kind Teacher* and the *Kind News* magazines. Send a self-addressed, stamped envelope for a free copy.

• Your teacher can write to the **Massachusetts Society for the Prevention of Cruelty to Animals** (**MSPCA**), 350 South Huntington Ave., Boston, MA 02130, for a $15 class subscription to *Children's Action for Animals* poster magazine. Designed for grades three to seven, the poster comes out three times a year.

● Borrow or buy the twenty-minute videotape *Kept in the Dark,* about a class of British school kids who learn the difference between "open air" and "factory" farming. You can borrow it for a $15 refundable deposit from **PETA,** P.O. Box 42516, Washington, DC 20015, or buy it for £12.50 (that's British pounds, about $18.75:see appendix B) from **Compassion in World Farming,** 20 Lavant St., Petersfield, Hampshire GU32 3EW, England (be sure to ask for the tape in U.S. format, "NTSC").

● Your class can "adopt" a wolf for $35 at **Wolf Haven America,** 3111 Offut Lake Rd., Tenino, WA 98589, a sanctuary that provides care and protection for these animals. You will receive a photograph of and adoption certificate for the wolf whose life you help to improve. You will also receive a subscription to the sanctuary's newsletter. For more ideas on helping wolves, write to **Friends of the Wolf,** 357½, Fremont N #7, Seattle, WA 98103. This group tries to stop wolf hunts and goes to court to fight for the wolves' freedom.

34 | HOORAY FOR HOLIDAYS!

On the first day of summer vacation, a duck, a frog, and a skunk decided to go to the movies. The duck got in because he had a bill, so did the frog because he had a greenback. But the skunk only had a scent and had to wait outside!

Everybody likes vacations, holidays, and special occasions. We can remember the animals at special times, too. Sometimes there are so many other things going on that we tend to forget them, but animals can make our celebrations that much more joyous.

DID YOU KNOW?

- If a cockroach got cards from all her sons and daughters on Mother's Day, she could have over three hundred of them!
- On October 5, Catholics celebrate Saint Francis Day. Saint Francis of Assisi is the patron saint of animals.

WHAT YOU CAN DO

- On Valentine's Day, remember your companion animals with a warm hug and a kiss. Send valentines to the animals and the people who work at your local animal shelter.
- If people you know are thinking of giving or getting chicks or baby rabbits in honor of Easter (or any other holiday), let them know that humane societies end up with lots of these animals, not always in great shape, *after* the holidays. Tell them plush animal toys or flowering plants (which require less care than animals) would be better.
- Think of companion animals on the Fourth of July, when they may be frightened by the sounds of firecrackers. It helps to sit with them, stroke them, talk to them quietly, and play soothing music on the radio to drown out bangs. You can also teach a timid dog not to be frightened by loud noises. Choose a special word or phrase to say to your dog each time there's a loud noise (like thunder). Say it in a really upbeat way—with the same tone of voice you would use to say, "Isn't this great?" Once you get your dog to respond to you (with a wag of the tail or whatever), praise him or her lavishly. It won't be long before your dog realizes those loud noises are kind of fun after all.
- Raccoons love Halloween so much, they wear their masks all year! This Halloween, dress up as an animal. What would it be like to have an elephant's long trunk or a polar bear's thick coat? Do you need to practice a new way of walking on four "legs" or holding things in your "paws"? You could hold or wear a sign with an animal rights message.
- This Thanksgiving, ask your parents if your family can enjoy a vegetarian meal and give thanks for *life* in all its wonderful forms. Did you know that in the wild (where turkeys are brown or black, not white), they can run up to eighteen miles per hour and fly even faster; and that turkeys flatten themselves against trees to fool hunters? You'll never miss munching on turkey when you can enjoy corn chowder, tofu loaf, harvest stuffing, and pumpkin pie instead.

• The next time you're in the market for a birthday, Christmas, or Hanukkah gift, think about buying some cruelty-free lotions, a toy that has not been tested on animals, a nonleather belt, or gourmet vegetarian foods. For the person who has everything, make a · donation in her or his name to an organization that helps animals.

• Get your school or family to celebrate Arbor Day (usually the last Friday in April) by planting a tree. In a year or two someone will have made a home in it! You can choose a tree, like an evergreen or spruce, that will make a good home for sparrows, finches, and starlings; or a food shrub, like a viburnum, whose fruits will provide winter meals for local wildlife. Squirrels, raccoons, possums, moths, worms, and frogs are some of the many animals that might eventually make a home in the tree you plant.

• Take out your calendar and add some new holidays:

  • Your animal friend's birthday! If you aren't sure of the date, pick one and celebrate it every year as you would any family birthday.
  • The Great American Meat-Out (March 21). Every year, animal rights groups encourage people to give up meat for a day (or a lifetime!) and see how easy it is. Try some of the foods described in chapters 23 and 36.
  • World Week for Animals in Laboratories (the fourth week in April). During this week, people all over the world hold rallies, give speeches, and meet to educate others about what happens to animals in laboratories.

• Check with local animal rights groups about any activities they may have planned for special days.

• If you know of someone who is getting married soon, you can give a gift to the couple that is really for the birds! Cut up squares of pretty fabric and put a handful of birdseed in each square. Then tie up the squares with colorful ribbon to make little sacks. Save them to distribute to the guests when the couple is about to leave, so that people can empty the birdseed into their hands and throw it over the newlyweds—instead of rice, which can swell up inside birds' stomachs and make them sick.

CHECK IT OUT

- For holiday recipes, write to the **Vegetarian Resource Group,** Box 1463, Baltimore, MD 21203; **Vegetarian Times,** P.O. Box 570, Oak Park, IL 60303; or **PETA,** P.O. Box 42516, Washington, DC 20015.

- See chapter 28 for the address of an organization that will send you a tree starting kit for a dollar.

- Write to or call **Seventh Generation,** Colchester, VT 05446–1672, 1-800-456-1177, for a catalog of environmentally friendly gifts, or to **PETA** for a catalog of cruelty-free and animal rights merchandise.

- Look at books on how to make costumes. Peggy Parish's *Costumes to Make* (Macmillan, 1970) has a six-page section devoted to animal costumes. Goldie Taub Chernoff's *Easy Costumes You Don't Have to Sew* (Scholastic Book Services, 1975) includes illustrated instructions for making many animal costumes such as mice, lions, lobsters, and chickens. Your library might have similar books on hand.

- Read *The Christmas Cat*, written by Efner Tudor Holmes and illustrated by Tasha Tudor (Crowell, New York, 1976). Appropriate for kids in elementary school.

- Flip to chapter 48, "School's Out!" for a list of great summer camps and day programs especially designed for kids who care about the animals and the Earth.

35 DRESSING COOL TO BE KIND

Ducks can feel pain,
so can cows, snakes, and sheep;
so why take body parts
that the animals should keep?
Animal products are never cool,
whether they're leather,
silk, down, or wool.
 —**LISA WOODCOCK,** age ten

Fur is not the only clothing made at the expense of animals. Leather, down, silk, and wool can cause animal suffering, too.

DID YOU KNOW?

- Most leather is cow skin. Many people who kill animals for meat also run their own leather tanneries. Talk about greedy—factory farmers have said they make a profit from every part of the cow except the "moo"!

- To turn animal skins into leather, tanners use substances such as formaldehyde that are harmful to us and to the environment. These substances give leather its funny smell.

- Leather also comes from horses, pigs, and lambs who are killed for food. But some animals, including mules, turtles, snakes, zebras, and kangaroos, are killed just for their skin! When you see a fancy leather handbag, belt, or pair of cowboy boots, tell the wearer that up to a third of "exotic" leathers come from illegally killed endangered animals.

- Wool is the sheared coat of sheep. If you get cold in the winter without your coat, imagine how shaved (or shorn) sheep feel—sheep whose wool has gone to market feel the cold even more than we humans do when we're naked!

- Sheep breeders have created a special type of sheep called merinos, who produce unnaturally large amounts of wool because their skin is very wrinkled. The overload of wool causes millions of them to die of the heat every summer. The extra wrinkles also cause another problem: maggot infestation. So, in order to prevent maggots, the sheep breeders actually cut away the flesh around and under the sheep's tail. This is extremely painful and takes a long time to heal.

- Silk comes from the shiny fiber that silkworms make for their cocoons. To take the silk from the silkworm, the silkworms have to be boiled or steamed alive in their cocoons. If someone asks, "Who cares?" just answer, "The silkworms do, so I do, too!"

- Down is the insulating feather coat of ducks and geese. Down feathers come from birds who have been killed (to make pâté, for example) or are pulled from living animals' bodies—not just once, but, in some countries, four or five times during their lives. Pulling out their feathers must hurt at least as much as it hurts us to pull out our eyebrow hairs. Down is out!

WHAT YOU CAN DO

- The Flintstones may have had to wear animal-based clothing, but today's smart fashions are kind to animals. Choose clothing made

from plant-based fibers such as cotton, canvas, ramie, and linen—
and from synthetic (human-made) materials such as acrylic, rayon,
and polyester. Many of your clothes are probably made from these
materials anyway. Tell your parents about the materials you want
to wear before the next time you go shopping.

- Be sure to avoid wallets, belts, watchbands, soccer balls, and any
other products made of leather. Instead, buy nylon wallets, metal
or plastic watchbands, plastic or cotton belts, and vinyl balls. If
you get a gift made of wool, down, silk, or leather, consider asking
the gift giver to exchange it for something not made from animals.

- "When you realize that the shoes you are wearing were once a
cow's hide, at least for me, I just can't do it," says champion
skateboarder Mike Vallely. Kindness is a shoe-in: give the boot
to cruelty by getting comfortable, attractive shoes made without
leather. Try synthetic running shoes from **Nike** or **New Balance**
or canvas all-purpose shoes from **Naturalizer** or **Hush Puppies;**
and, of course, don't forget your rubber boots! When you're shopping, ask the salesperson for help if you're not sure what's made
of what.

- Instead of down, follow the lead of most mountain climbers and
choose a coat made of Polyguard or Thinsulate. These synthetic
materials keep you warmer and drier than down. If you have a
down comforter, pillow, and other feathery items, when they wear
out, replace them with something that won't bring you (or the
birds) down.

- Advertise! Rock singer Lene Lovich stitches sequins or studs on
her big belts to spell out "FAKE!"

CHECK IT OUT

- For a good selection of nonleather, synthetic, and fabric shoes,
visit a **Payless Shoe Store** or write for catalogs to:

  • **Aesop Unlimited,** Department 304, P.O. Box 315, Cambridge,
  MA 02140
  • **Heartland Products, Ltd.,** Box 218, Dakota City, IA 50529
  (enclose $1)

- A nonleather softball, in both white and fluorescent colors, is available from **Spalding.** Call them for free at 1-800-642-5004 for more information.
- To find the store nearest you that sells **Nike** nonleather sneakers, call 1-800-344-NIKE.
- **Patagonia,** 1609 West Babcock St., P.O. Box 8900, Bozeman, MT 59715-2046, makes a lot of attractive, warm, non-animal-derived active-wear clothes, including a nonchinchilla "synchilla" jacket! Call 1-800-336-9090 to ask for the latest catalog.

36 | PIG OUT

Question: When is a hot dog not a hot dog?
Answer: When it's a Tofu Pup!

DID YOU KNOW?

- Tofu Pups are made out of tofu, which is made from soybeans. Soybeans can be processed and shaped into all kinds of foods that look and taste just like the things lots of new vegetarians might miss. Hot dogs, hamburgers, cold cuts, ice cream, milk, and anything else you can imagine can be made out of soybeans or other beans, grains, or vegetables.
- In 1989, Candlestick Park in San Francisco, California, started selling Tofu Pups to baseball fans.
- Comedian Steve Martin insists on nonmeat ''dogs'' at the ballpark and at home, and so can you.
- Meat hot dogs are made out of pigs, cows, or turkeys. Soy products are made out of beans and so are better for you *and* the animals.

- Pigs are very smart and clean animals who can communicate with us just as well as, if not better than, dogs can. Pigs cared for by people who enjoy their company (and not the way they taste!) learn to understand many human words, become housebroken, and show much affection to their human friends. Pigs are very joyful animals when not kept in tiny stalls on factory farms.
- Cows and bulls are vegetarians. On factory farms their babies are taken away from them after only a day or two. They are not allowed to enjoy being outside, and they're shipped in dark, crowded trucks to sheds to be killed for hamburgers or "all-beef franks."
- Turkeys raised for lunch meat and turkey franks have a terrible time on today's factory farms, too. They are kept in such cramped conditions that farmers cut their beaks off so they don't hurt each other out of frustration. They are bred to have such big bodies that their legs give out under the weight.

WHAT YOU CAN DO

- You can save pigs, cows, and turkeys by eating Tofu Pups instead of hot dogs. Tofu Pups are made by **Tempeh Works** and are sold at many health food stores.
- Bring Tofu Pups to cookouts and share them with everyone.
- For lunch, pack a Foney Baloney sandwich. You can find **Light-life**'s Foney Baloney at many health food stores.
- **Worthington Foods'** Loma Linda division makes meatless hot dogs called "Big Franks" and "Sizzle Links," as well as vegetarian burgers and other meatless foods. Call their toll-free number, 1-800-628-3663, to ask where their foods are sold near your house.
- **Nobull Foods** makes a snack called "Fib Ribs." They are made out of wheat gluten and are smothered in barbecue sauce. Perfect for an afternoon snack! If your local health food store doesn't carry Fib Ribs, call 1-800-828-7648 to find out where you can buy some.
- Write a letter to the manager of your local grocery store asking her or him to carry these products. Ask your friends to write, too. Make copies of the list of some good vegetarian food companies (you can write to **PETA** for suggestions), and give a copy to all the local grocery store managers. Meanwhile, look for these foods at the health food store, and happy chowing down!

• Everyone knows slaughterhouses are ugly places, but since many people can't imagine *not* eating animals, they don't want to think about what happened to their dinner when it was still an animal. Learn how animals are raised on factory farms, how they are transported, and how they are killed. The facts aren't pretty, but knowing them will help you stick up for the animals and stick to your new diet. (See chapter 23, "Try It, You'll Like It," for some books and pamphlets you can buy, borrow, or send away for.)

• Don't be a meat addict! Eat for life: your own life (since meat is high in fat and cholesterol, it is unhealthy as well as inhumane) and the animals' lives.

CHECK IT OUT

• Send a self-addressed, stamped envelope to **Nobull Foods,** 6987 N. Oracle Rd., Suite 105, Tucson, AZ 85704, for a free sample of their Fib Ribs (yum!).

37 TAKE CARE OF HOT DOGS

Do you know a dog who wears a coat and pants? You probably do, so help keep him or her from getting hot under the collar! In the summer, the temperature inside a car can get hot enough to fry an egg, but a dog in a hot car is no "yoke."

DID YOU KNOW?

- When the temperature is above 70° F, the inside of a parked car can reach 120° to 175° F within minutes—*even with the windows cracked.*

  - Even in the shade, a hot car can quickly become an oven.
  - Even if the car air-conditioning was on until you left the car, hot air swiftly replaces the cold.
  - Animals left in cars can suffer serious, sometimes fatal, heat stroke.

149

- Dogs "sweat" only through their footpads and their mouths, by panting.

WHAT YOU CAN DO

- Never leave an animal in a parked car in warm weather, even for a few minutes.
- Watch for animals left in cars in parking lots on hot days.

  - If you see one, immediately call the police, humane society, or animal control. Ask for help freeing the animal if she or he is panting heavily or collapsing.
  - If the car is outside a large store, ask the manager to make an announcement over the loudspeaker.
  - Pour cold water from a nearby business or public restroom over an animal to lower his or her temperature and hopefully save his or her life.

- Get a supply of "Don't Park the Dog" fliers and put them on windshields in shopping centers and around the neighborhood during warm weather. Ask your local animal shelter or PETA for some.
- Call radio stations and ask them to make "Hot Dog Warning" public service announcements (PSAs).
- Show shopping mall managers the facts on your fliers, and ask them to have stores in the mall set out "Please Take One" holders for your fliers.

  - You can offer to supply the holders. Clean half-gallon beverage cartons decorated with contact paper, with the top and front cut out, are easy and fun to make.
  - Ask the mall managers to announce over the PA system several times a day that animal protection agencies will break a window or door lock, if necessary, to get an animal out of a car.

CHECK IT OUT

- Call your local TV stations and ask if they will air a thirty-second videotape called "Hot Dog" about dogs in parked cars. Make a list of willing stations (and their addresses), and send it to **PETA,** P.O. Box 42516, Washington, DC 20015. PETA will send a free copy of the video to every station that wants one.

38 OH, DEER!

Wouldn't it be awful, wouldn't it be queer,
To be playing in the woods and be shot by a deer?
To be strolling with friends in the afternoon sun,
Just to be stopped by some deer with a gun,
And blasted to bits while out having some fun?
So consider this thought and remember it clear,
It wouldn't be fun to be shot by a deer.

—PETE TRAYNOR

Some people kill animals like deer and call it "sport," but a sport is an activity that involves people who *want* to play the game. **The Fund for Animals** points out how unfair hunting is with a bumper sticker that reads "Support Your Right to Arm Bears!"

DID YOU KNOW?

- Every year, hunters in the United States kill more than 200 million animals, not to mention quite a few people killed or wounded when shot by mistake. That is more than twice as many animals as there are people in California (24 million), New York (18 million), Illinois (11 million), Michigan (9 million), Ohio (11 million), Pennsylvania (12 million), and Texas (15 million) put together!
- Many hunters use ''calls'' that mimic animals in distress, then blast away when other animals come to the rescue.
- Some hunters say that if they don't kill animals in autumn, the animals will starve during the winter, yet animals were here long before people were, and they did fine without being hunted. In fact, in places where hunting is legal, animal populations actually *grow* every year and more animals starve there than in places where hunting is against the law. Also, there is no way for hunters to know whether or not the animals they killed would have been ones who starved. In fact, hunters try to shoot big, healthy animals— the ones who have the best chance at making it through the winter.
- Only 7 percent of Americans hunt. The majority of people in the United States enjoy seeing free-roaming animals *alive*.
- Some people who want animals to live unharmed try to disrupt hunts by putting human hair from barber shops (or even lion's dung from the zoo) around trees where hunters build platforms. The smell alerts animals to the presence of the enemy.

WHAT YOU CAN DO

Here are some ideas to help the animals who live in the woods near you:

- If you live in the country, make big signs that say ''NO HUNT-ING'' and hang them on trees and fences all over your property. Get your friends to do the same.
- Some pieces of land have been set aside for animals. These are called ''national wildlife refuges'' and were meant to be safe places

for animals to live. While people can't build houses on the refuges, some refuges allow people to hunt on them. Write to your congressperson to protest hunting on national wildlife refuges (you can find out who your congressperson is at your local library). Send your letter to the **House of Representatives,** Washington, DC 20515, or to the **United States Senate,** Washington, DC 20510. Your letter can be short and sharp, like the following:

The Honorable Mary Smith
The U.S. Senate
Washington, DC 20510

Dear Senator Smith,

What good are national wildlife refuges to the animals? People hunt and trap there. It is a shame because the animals have no place to be safe. Please make our national wildlife refuges the safe places they were meant to be by making hunting and trapping in them illegal.

Sincerely,
[name]

- Write to the **U.S. Fish and Wildlife Service,** U.S.F.W.S. Publications, MS ARLSQ 130, 1800 C St., N.W., Washington, DC 20240, for a free color map showing where national wildlife refuges are in the United States.
- If people in your family hunt, try to persuade them to carry a camera rather than a gun into the woods. Animals ''shot'' with a camera can still go home at night to take care of their babies.

CHECK IT OUT

- Send $1.50 to **The Fund for Animals,** 200 W. 57th St., Suite 508, New York, NY 10019, for the ''Arm Bears'' bumper sticker and ask for a copy of their pamphlet, *Armchair Activist*, which describes more things you can do for the animals.

- Write to **Friends of Animals,** P.O. Box 1244, Norwalk, CT 06856, for their "Exploding Myths About Hunting" poster (ten for $1).

- Join the **Foxcubs,** P.O. Box 1, Carlton, Nottingham NG4 2JY, England, the kids' section of the British group called Hunt Saboteurs Association. For £3 (that's British pounds, approximately $5), you'll receive an information pack and four newsletters a year, including stories, quizzes, and features about animals and the countryside. Or you can send for free information about hunted animals or about becoming a vegetarian.

- Write to **PETA,** P.O. Box 42516, Washington, DC 20015, for a free postcard to spread the word about hunting to a friend.

39 GIVE A WELL-COME GIFT

If anyone calls you a drip,
Say, "a drip is a drop,
A drop is water,
Water is nature,
And nature is beautiful!"
—**KAREN PRATT,** age eight

To get a drink of clean water, most people just turn on a tap. Imagine if there was no running water and you didn't live near a river! That's what it's like for many little animals who live in the city and can't turn on the water faucets themselves. If you watch birds after a good rain, you can see them drinking little raindrops off the tips of leaves. But what do they do when it hasn't rained for a while?

Since birds and other beings who live in the city must drink to survive, they seek out any little puddles of water they can find. Cracks and dips in the pavement can hold water after it has rained, but look at the water:

it can be shiny with motor oil or full of trash. Drinking it could be hazardous to anyone's health, but sometimes there's no choice.

DID YOU KNOW?

- Animal bodies, including yours, are 98 percent water.
- A camel can drink up to thirty gallons of water at one time!
- The only rodent who doesn't drink water is a kind of desert rat called the kangaroo rat. Kangaroo rats get all the water they need by eating the juicy leaves of desert plants.

WHAT YOU CAN DO

Turn on the tap for those who can't:

- Turn a shallow baking pan into a birdbath to allow feathered beings to splash around and cool down on hot days. Hint: Water pans must always be kept clean and should never be more than two inches deep, or birds, especially young ones, can slip in and not be able to get out again. Change the water every day.
- Clean out trash from watering holes in the pavement or in other places where birds and other animals may drink.
- Trees need a drink, too. A healthy tree is a living home for lots of animals. Dump a pan of water at the base of a tree "house" in dry weather. Turn on the garden hose and/or sprinkler for plants and trees.
- Look out for dogs on chains and rabbits in hutches; they need water bowls with fresh water daily. Ask your neighbors for permission to secure water bowls in tires or onto a fence to avoid spills or to weigh the bowls down with clean rocks or a brick.
- Scrub out and refill water bowls at home, too. For little animals like hamsters, mice, and guinea pigs who use bottles, make sure the bottles are clean and their necks unclogged. And leave a little bowl of water, too, for safety's sake.

CHECK IT OUT

- For more ideas, write to **PETA,** P.O. Box 42516, Washington, DC 20015, for a free brochure called *10 Easy Ways to Prevent Animal Suffering*.

CRITTER CHATTER

When addressing a horse
Is your language too coarse?
Could you use your lingo
In front of a dingo?

        —ANONYMOUS

DID YOU KNOW?

Words we say, hear, and read have a powerful effect on us and how we see others. Sometimes people develop bad feelings about animals simply from the words they choose. For example, we insult people by calling them names like "pig" or "goose," when pigs are really very smart and friendly (in ancient times they were considered sacred), and geese love their families and protect them, even in the face of grave personal danger.

WHAT YOU CAN DO

- In school or at a party or get-together, see who can write down the most names of animals that people use to insult each other. Then write down those animals' good points beside their names. Next, pledge to stop using names of animals as insults and use them as compliments instead!

- What's wrong with this sentence? "The dog was hungry, so I fed it." If you're tuned in to how language is misused when animals are involved, you'll show your respect for other-than-human beings by calling them "he" or "she," "someone" (not "something"), and never "it." "It" refers to things, not living beings. If you're not sure, just say "she or he" or "he or she."

- Don't say "which" or "that" when referring to an animal. Say, for example, "The animal *who* came to our house . . ."

- Avoid ugly expressions like "kill two birds with one stone," "wear kid gloves," or "make a silk purse out of a sow's ear." Get out of the habit by making a beeper noise whenever you catch yourself or a friend saying negative things about animals!

- Instead of "pet," say "friend," "companion," or "companion animal" ("companimal"!), and say "friend," "guardian," "companion," or "protector" instead of "owner" or "master." Animals aren't our property, they're our friends.

- Write to the editor of your local newspaper and ask him or her to refer to animals in the paper as "he" or "she" (or "s/he," which you can write but can't pronounce), not "it."

- Ask your teacher to please have the class refer to animals as individuals, not objects, and to describe other-than-human beings in positive ways. Suggest a class discussion about referring to animals properly, so that others will realize the need.

- Stop fooling yourself by calling the flesh of dead animals "meat," "veal," "pork," or "poultry." Start saying "cows," "calves," "pigs," "chickens," and "turkeys." Remembering where bits of food came from makes us think about what—or whom—we eat.

- If you hear someone say, "He acted like an animal," remind him or her it's usually *humans* who wage wars, steal, cheat, and act spitefully toward each other. And anyway, we human beings are just another type of animal—that's a biological fact!

CHECK IT OUT

- Spend some time reading a magazine or newspaper and underline wording that wrongly refers to an animal as "it" or "which" or that depicts animals in unflattering ways or promotes cruelties like hunting.

PRODUCE A PLAY

...friends, Romans, countrymen, lend me your ears....

Question: How did the playwright get a standing ovation?
Answer: She sold all the chairs.

Question: When is a stage door not a stage door?
Answer: When it's ajar.

Question: And when is theater humor not very funny?
Answer: When it's simply a play on words.

When a fourth-grade class in Milton, Massachusetts, performed the play *Charlotte's Web,* adapted from the novel by E. B. White, a reporter and photographer from the local newspaper came to the school to interview and photograph students on stage and behind the scenes. Their story in the *Milton Record-Transcript* helped draw attention to animals as individuals and to the plight of animals raised as food.

DID YOU KNOW?

- A play is a wonderful way to spread the word about kindness to animals and is fun for the people on stage, backstage, and in the audience.
- A play can be performed many times for different audiences.
- A play is a great way to put lots of people's different talents to work for the animals.

WHAT YOU CAN DO

- Write your own play. Here are some ideas of what it could be about:

  • Animals in a laboratory or pet store, or animals sent to be in a circus.
  • Animals in the forest as hunting and trapping season approaches.
  • Animals who escape from a farm where they were being raised for meat.
  • Animals who get lost and end up at an animal shelter.
  • Birds who escape from cages and get to fly for the first time in their lives and be with each other after being alone.
  • Any good animal story you've heard or read that you could adapt into a play.

- Put on a play someone else has written, such as *The Trapper,* by beaver expert Hope Buyukmihci. Beavers are delightful, friendly, and interesting animals who do wonderful things for the environment.
- Get pictures of the kinds of animals in your play and think of ideas for costumes.

- You can design and make your own costumes. To make a cat costume, for example, you can use a leotard and tights. Make the tail and neck ruff from fake fur, another fuzzy material, or rope.
- Maybe you can also borrow costumes from a school, local club, or church.

• You can either paint faces on with makeup, make masks, or make animal heads.

- Concentrate on the eyes and whiskers of the animal face you are painting.
- To make a simple rat mask, use a paper cone, Ping-Pong ball, and piece of elastic. Marker or spray-paint the Ping-Pong ball gray, black, or pink, make a hole in it to fit the small end of the cone, and stick it on. Stick pipe cleaners or drinking straws into the cone for whiskers. You can make ears and attach them to a hat or headband. Make a small hole on either side of the wide end of the cone, then thread the ends of the elastic through and knot them.
- Using the same basic idea and instructions, you can use different colors of paper and sizes of cones to make different kinds of animals with pointy faces, such as foxes, bears, or birds. For a bird, leave off the Ping-Pong ball and draw a line down either side of the cone to show the beak.

• To make an animal head mask, mold chicken wire into the shape of an animal head (you'll need adult help for this; it's a little more complicated). Make holes for eyes, so you can see when you're wearing it. Carefully try it on for size.

- Cut or tear up newspapers into two- or three-inch strips. Soak them in wallpaper glue. Put them onto the frame in layers. Leave the eye holes clear.
- You can mold the layers into shapes while they're wet.
- Let the head dry overnight, then paint it. If you use a water-based paint (check the container), let it dry and then apply several coats of varnish to make it waterproof.

- You can make a curtain out of an old pair of drapes or two bedsheets or blankets.
- Can someone videotape your play? This way, it will always be available to classmates, elementary schools, and civic clubs and churches—and you can improve on your play by watching the tape!
- Let teachers know your play is available. One or two of the actors can answer questions after the performance or video.
- You might also ask the children's librarian at your public library if she or he would like to have a performance or video showing for a Saturday children's program. (Here, too, one or two actors should stay to answer questions following the play.)
- Instead of a stage play, use a video camera to make your own TV show (you could put in ads for cruelty-free products!) or movie.

CHECK IT OUT

- Maybe your teacher or camp counselor will let the class or group put on a play about animals, or you and others can do it on your own. You can invite your parents and friends. Perhaps you can charge a small admission fee and donate this to your local humane society or another group that helps animals.
- For Hope Buyukmihci's play about beavers, *The Trapper*, write to her at **Unexpected Wildlife Refuge,** P.O. Box 765, Newfield, NJ 08344. Please send 50¢ to cover printing and mailing costs.
- Look over the books listed in chapter 43 for a story you might want to adapt into a play.
- Check out costume books from your library. *Easy Costumes You Don't Have to Sew,* by Goldie Taub Chernoff and Margaret A. Hartelius, is especially good. (Also see costume books listed in chapter 34, ''Hooray for Holidays!'')
- Those who are shy—or who have less space to work with—can put on a puppet show instead of a play.

42 | PACK A LUNCH WITH A PUNCH

Can you imagine being locked in a classroom in semidarkness, unable to move from your desk, turn around, or even go to the restroom—for months on end!

Now you've an idea what factory farms are like.

—School Campaign for Reaction Against Meat (SCREAM),
The Vegetarian Society of the U.K.

Lunchtime is a great time to promote kindness to animals. After all, we make life-and-death decisions for animals (and ourselves) at the lunch counter every day. Let your friends and classmates know that they can vote yes to life by "eating veggie" for lunch.

DID YOU KNOW?

● Lunches offered at most schools today are full of grease, or animal fat, which is very bad for us. Purely vegetarian foods are much lower in fat than animal foods and don't have any cholesterol in them at all.

- A study of 6,500 people between the ages of three and eighteen showed that many young people have high levels of cholesterol, which can cause heart attacks and other health problems later on in life. High cholesterol can be caused by eating too much fat and too many animal products like meat, eggs, and dairy products.

- Hunzas, people who live in the Himalayan mountains in Pakistan, eat almost no animal products. Most of these people live to be at least one hundred years old, dancing and singing on their one hundredth birthdays!

- Because so many dolphins have been killed in drift nets set out to catch tuna, students in Milford, Connecticut, and Aurora, Colorado, got their schools to take tuna off their lunch menus. By talking to your principal or food service director, circulating a petition, or holding an assembly about how animals are raised for food, your group can try to get veal taken off—and tofu added to—your school's menu.

- The Vegetarian Society gave a school cook in England some money so that he could offer and promote meatless meals. He used the money to buy posters and menu boards to promote vegetarianism at the school. He also had a "design a sticker with a vegetarian message" contest at the school, which only people who bought the vegetarian meal at lunch could enter. Some comments from the students were "I think the veggie burgers and lasagna were nice—I tried them because of the cruelty to animals in making meat" and "It's great that we have a choice now. I liked the pancakes best. I'm not a vegetarian now, but I will be when I leave home!" The head cook at the school said, "The promotion was more successful than we anticipated. We will be pleased to provide more vegetarian meals from now on."

- Paul McCartney, who was in the Beatles rock band and whom many consider to be the most successful musician ever, brings a vegetarian chef with him on tour. No meat is allowed backstage at the concerts, and anyone caught eating it there is thrown out!

WHAT YOU CAN DO

- Since you probably can't take a vegetarian chef with you to school every day, work to get more (and tastier) meatless dishes and meals served in your lunchroom—after all, you can't live on green beans and Tater Tots alone! There are lots of easy-to-make foods such as veggie burgers, Tofu Pups, and vegetarian chili. Let the cooks in the cafeteria know your many reasons for not wanting to eat meat. Encourage other kids to speak to them, too.
- If you have difficulty getting your school to agree to serve vegetarian meals and/or options, ask your parents to speak to the principal.
- Ask other kids and parents to sign a petition. Even people who aren't vegetarian can agree that a choice should be available for those who don't eat meat. Some of most people's favorite foods are already vegetarian, like spaghetti with tomato sauce.
- If you still have trouble convincing the cafeteria to offer vegetarian meals, write a letter to the school newspaper to inform your classmates and encourage students to support your efforts. After all, vegetarian meals would benefit everyone!
- Don't give up! It may take time to get meatless meals on the menu at your school, but if you keep working, others will understand and join you.
- While you're campaigning for healthy meals at school, you may want to "brown bag it." Peanut butter and jelly on whole-grain bread, falafel or soy "meat" sandwiches (see chapter 36 for more information), fruit salad, and trail mix are just a few of the healthy foods you can take to school for lunch.

CHECK IT OUT

- Write to the **Physicians Committee for Responsible Medicine (PCRM),** P.O. Box 6322, Washington, DC 20015, for their complete plan for healthy cafeteria lunches. This group of doctors and health experts will be happy to help you work with your school.

- Write to **CHOICE!,** The Vegetarian Society, Parkdale, Dunham Rd., Altrincham, Cheshire WA14 4QG, England, for information about how young vegetarians in England work to get more meatless meals in their school cafeterias. You can order a "4-Week Menu Planner." (complete with "57 imaginative, tasty, and nutritionally well-balanced recipes in an easy-to-read format") for £3.50 (that's $6.50), nutritional guidelines for £1, and a stand-up, write-on, wipe-off menu board with the wording "Vegetarian Dish of the Day" for £7.50 (or $14.00).

- Write to **PETA,** P.O. Box 42516, Washington, DC 20015, for a free button to wear to school. Let people know you'd like a "Meat-Free America" or that "Meat Stinks"—and tell them why!

43 BE A BOOKWORM

Question: Who helps a bookworm read at night?
Answer: A lightning bug!

Chip couldn't believe it. The man sitting in front of him at the movies had his arm around a huge dog. The dog was staring at the screen, snarling and growling and showing his teeth.

Chip tapped the man on the shoulder. "I'm amazed. Your dog really hates this movie."

The man turned around and said, "Frankly, I'm surprised, too. He *loved* the book."

Books are wonderful companions. They let a chicken tell why she likes to scratch in the dirt or a dog explain the relief of having a thorn pulled out of his paw. This chapter lists some terrific books about animals and our relationships with them. Your school or local library probably has some of them already; ask your teacher or librarian to help you get the others. Maybe you can get a copy of your own for your birthday or save up to buy one for yourself.

DID YOU KNOW?

- Humans aren't the only ones to use tools. Sea otters use stones as hammers. Finches on the Galápagos Islands use a cactus spine or a sharp twig as a fork. Chimpanzees sometimes crumple leaves to make a sponge so they can get drinking water trapped in places they otherwise couldn't.
- The male regent bowerbird paints with a brush and natural colors. Mixing saliva with earth color, plant pigments, and charcoal, he dips a piece of bark or a wadded leaf in the paint and creates green or blue-gray murals in his living space.
- Honeybees dance to communicate with their sisters. Like us, they speak in symbols. For example, when a forager bee returns to the hive to tell her sisters she has found a good place to get nectar and pollen, she runs in a figure eight. The other bees can tell how far away the place is by how long she runs. In one species of honeybee, running for one second means the nectar is five hundred kilometers from the hive, and a two-second run means they'll only have to go two kilometers from the hive.
- You can learn all these things and more from reading books.

WHAT YOU CAN DO

- Look in your library and bookstores for books that tell more about the special characteristics and behaviors of other-than-human animals, such as *My Life with the Chimpanzees,* by Jane Goodall (Pocket/Minstrel, 1988; ages eight to sixteen).
- Order a guide that describes and recommends books for children up through age seven that promote concern for other beings and the environment. This long list also tells which books treat animals badly. Order the guide from **Amberwood,** Rt. 1, Box 206, Milner, GA 30257 ($3 plus $1 postage).

CHECK 'EM OUT!

The books listed below are in alphabetical order by author, with titles for younger readers at the end of each category.

Classics

- *Lassie Come Home,* Eric Knight (Harmony, Raine, and Co., Greenport, NY, 1981). First published in 1940, this is the touching story of a collie's love for her human friend.
- *My Friend Flicka,* Mary O'Hara (Harper & Row/Eyre and Spottiswoode, London, 1943). A boy gains maturity through caring for a young horse.
- *The Yearling,* Marjorie Rawlings (Charles Scribner's Sons, New York, 1938; new edition by Collier Books). A boy adopts a baby deer, and the deer causes trouble for his family.
- *Beautiful Joe,* Marshall Saunders, retold by Quinn Currie (Storytellers Ink, Seattle, WA, 1990). First written in 1893, this is the remarkable true story of a rescued dog born in a stable on the outskirts of a small town in Maine.
- *Black Beauty,* Anna Sewell (first published in 1877; new edition by Storytellers Ink, Seattle, WA). A horse is passed from "owner" to "owner," encountering both the good and the bad of humanity.
- *The Hundred and One Dalmatians,* Dodie Smith (Penguin, New York, 1956). When Dalmatians begin disappearing all over the country, it is up to a Dalmatian couple and their puppies to solve the mystery.
- *The Red Pony,* John Steinbeck (Penguin, New York, 1959). A coming-of-age novel about a boy and a pony.
- *Charlotte's Web,* E. B. White (Harper & Row and Dell, 1952). How Charlotte the spider and farm girl Fern work together to save Wilbur the pig from slaughter.
- *Stuart Little,* E. B. White (Harper & Row, 1945). The adventures of a mouse living with a family of humans.
- *Frederick,* Leo Lionni (Pantheon, 1967). While the rest of his mouse family is busy gathering traditional supplies to get them

through the winter, Frederick tells them he is gathering things like sunshine and the colors of the meadows, which help them get through the winter. (For younger readers.)

- *Blueberries for Sal,* Robert McCloskey (The Viking Press, 1948 and 1976). The sweet story of a little girl and a bear cub who mistakenly begin to follow each other's mothers while out picking blueberries. (Younger readers.)
- *Make Way for Ducklings,* Robert McCloskey (Viking, New York, 1941). The true story of how traffic was stopped in Boston, Massachusetts, to let a mother duck and her babies cross the street. (Younger readers.)

Nonfiction

- *Animals, Nature and Albert Schweitzer,* Ann Cottrell Free (The Flying Fox Press, Washington, D.C., 1988). A collection of writings by the Nobel Prize-winning doctor who proclaimed the ethic of reverence for all life.
- *I Love Animals and Broccoli,* Debra Wasserman and Charles Stahler (Vegetarian Resource Group, P.O. Box 1463, Baltimore, MD 21203). A book of games, puzzles, and stories about healthy eating and caring about animals.

Fiction

- *Who Will Speak for the Lamb?,* Mildred Ames (Harper & Row Junior Books, New York, 1989). With realistic characters, this story takes a stand for the rights of all other-than-human beings, especially those being kept in laboratories.
- *The Bollo Caper,* Art Buchwald, illustrations by Elise Primavera (G. P. Putnam's Sons, New York, 1983). Bollo, the most beautiful leopard in Africa, is trapped and brought to New York City to become a fur coat. He ends up in Washington, D.C., where he pushes along a bill to protect endangered species.
- *The Midnight Fox,* Betsy Byars (Viking, 1975). After Tom saw the fox he thought, "There is a great deal of difference between

seeing an animal in a zoo in front of painted fake rocks and trees and seeing one natural and free in the woods. It was like seeing a kite on the floor and then, later, seeing one up in the sky where it was supposed to be, pulling at the wind.''

- *Newberry: The Life and Times of a Maine Clam,* Vincent Dethier, illustrations by Marie Litterer (Down East Books, Camden, Maine, 1981). Entertaining story about the experiences of Newberry the clam when he leaves his comfortable mud flat to find help for a neck ache. Woven into the story are descriptions of the habits and behaviors of many marine animals living in the mud flats.
- *A Cat's Nine Lives,* Lilo Hess (Charles Scribner's Sons, New York, 1984). The trials and tribulations of Misty, a Persian cat who experiences many of the hazards and problems faced by cats in modern society. The author also shows the benefits of committing ourselves to caring for and loving our companion animals.
- *Much Ado About Aldo,* Johanna Hurwitz (Morrow, New York, 1978). Because of a school project, eight-year-old Aldo stops eating meat.
- *Perfect the Pig,* Susan Jeschke (Henry Holt & Co., 1981). The story of a winged pig shows in a humorous way what life is truly like for animals in the circus.
- *Come Again in the Spring,* Richard Kennedy, illustrations by Marcia Sewell (Harper, 1976). Old man Hark refuses to go when Death comes in winter. The birds have stayed north because he feeds them, and they will die if he goes. The birds help Hark in a wager with Death.
- *Martin's Mice,* Dick King-Smith (Crown Publishers Inc., New York, 1989). A story about a companion cat who keeps mice as his own companion animals.
- *The Mare on the Hill,* Thomas Locker (Dial Books, 1985). A beautiful story about a mare who has previously been abused and the two children who patiently gain her trust.
- *Mrs. Frisby and the Rats of NIMH,* Robert C. O'Brien (1971). The story of a brave mouse who seeks help from the mysterious and wise rats living nearby.
- *Winter Barn,* Peter Parnall (Macmillan, 1986). The story of a number of wild animals, each taking shelter in their own corner or crevice of an old barn as they survive the subzero winter of Maine, awaiting the first signs of spring.

- *Every Living Thing,* Cynthia Rylant (Bradbury Press, 1985). Twelve stories about the extraordinary relationships between human and other-than-human beings.
- *A Rat's Tale,* Tom Seidler (Farrar, Straus & Giroux, Inc., 1986). A witty novel with a rat's point of view about a peaceful kingdom.
- *Storm in the Night,* Mary Stolz, illustrated by Pat Cummings (Harper, 1988). A thunderstorm puts the lights out, and an African-American boy listens to his grandfather's tale of another storm long ago, a frightened boy, and a lost dog.
- *Hunter and His Dog,* Brian Wildsmith (Oxford University Press, Oxford, England, 1979). What happens when a hunter's dog cares for the injured animals instead of bringing them back to the hunter?
- *Hey! Get Off Our Train,* John Burningham (Crown Publishers, Inc., New York, 1989). The adventures of a little boy who goes on a train ride and finds endangered animal friends along the way. (For younger readers.)
- *Nathan's Fishing Trip,* Lulu Delacre (Scholastic Inc., New York, 1988). A mouse and an elephant learn what a fishing trip means for the fishes. (Younger readers.)

True Stories/Autobiography

- *The Cat Who Came for Christmas,* Cleveland Amory (Penguin, New York, 1988). The true story of how a New York City gentleman's life was changed by a cat named Polar Bear.
- *Kinship with All Life,* J. Allen Boone (Harper & Row, New York, 1954). Real-life stories about communications between animals of different species, including between humans and other animals.
- *The Incredible Journey,* Sheila Burnford (Little, Brown and Co., Boston, 1961). The true story of two dogs and a cat who travel together over two hundred miles of Canadian countryside to get home.
- *Arnie, the Darling Starling,* Margarete S. Corbo and Diane Marie Barras (Houghton Mifflin Co., Boston, 1983). A man cares for a starling who had fallen from his nest.
- *Friends of All Creatures,* Rose Evans (Sea Fog Press, San Francisco, CA, 1984). A look at how people through the ages have shown compassion for animals.

- *My Life with the Chimpanzees,* Jane Goodall (Pocket Books, 1988). The famous primatologist describes her adventures in getting to know the chimpanzees of Gombe, Africa.

44 REFLECTING ON DISSECTING

What a wonderful bird the frog are!
When he walk, he fly almost;
When he sing, he cry almost.
He ain't got no tail hardly, either.
He sit on what he ain't got almost.

—**ANONYMOUS**

Your teacher wants you to dissect. You decide to study:

A. A cat.
B. A rat.
C. A Ribbit.

What could be more painless than "dissecting" Ribbit—a cloth model frog? When you open the Ribbit frog's Velcro-fastened tummy, you see all the differently colored organs inside.

Like Tom Arnold, Advanced Placement biology teacher in Wheaton, Maryland, teachers all over the country have used Ribbit and/or other models, books, and computer programs to replace dissecting.

DID YOU KNOW?

● Almost six million animals are used in classroom dissection every year. We are taught we should love animals, but many schools still require students to dissect. It doesn't make sense to kill frogs, worms, cats, mice, and pigs to study their bodies—especially when there are so many other ways to learn.

● Lots of students just won't dissect.

• California high school student Jenifer Graham took her case all the way to the federal court and won her right to leave the animals alone. As a result, California passed a law that protects the rights of students in public schools to object to dissection. Her story was even made into an *After School Special* for television!

• Robert Michael, a Canadian student, asked his classmates and teacher to consider the cruelty of dissection. After Robert told them about the better and humane alternatives to dissection, all the students voted not to dissect, so they studied atoms and molecules instead. Robert also talked to the principal, who then talked to the other teachers about using alternatives to dissection.

• Kids all over the country are working together and with teachers, parents, and other supportive adults to get dissection out of their classrooms. There are lots of organizations willing to help. (See "Check It Out," below, for some of their names and addresses.)

WHAT YOU CAN DO

● Talk to your teacher. Explain that you care about animals and don't want to harm them. It's important for your teacher to understand that you're not trying to get out of the lesson simply because you think it's gross (although it is!) or that you don't want to do the work. There is a good chance he or she has a more interesting project that you can work on, but you might suggest one yourself.

● Chances are, others in your class don't feel comfortable cutting up animals and wish they had an alternative. Encourage them to speak up about their feelings. You might want to start a petition for the right to a "violence-free" education.

- Tell your parents how you feel—they can support you. Explain your reasons for objecting, and they're sure to understand!

- Check out the many alternatives, including computer models like Visifrog (available on Apple and Macintosh), models made of cloth or plastic, diagrams, books, filmstrips, and videotapes. Alternatives can be reused by students for years to come, they don't smell, and they don't get thrown out with the trash!

- If your teacher *insists* that you dissect, ask him or her to meet with you and your parents to discuss your concerns. If your instructor still won't budge, ask to meet with your principal.

CHECK IT OUT

- Contact animal protection groups that are ready to help you with free advice and information. Make a free phone call to the **Dissection Hotline** at 1-800-922-FROG. You'll talk to people who have refused to dissect and have all kinds of helpful advice.

- Write to **PETA**, P.O. Box 42516, Washington, DC 20015, for a free "Dissection Pack" that includes fact sheets on dissection and biological supply companies, lists and descriptions of alternatives, a model resolution allowing each student to decide whether or not to dissect, and other information. You can also order PETA's twenty-page report, "Dying for Biology" for $3 and fifteen-minute video, *Classroom Cut-Ups,* for $15 (or free thirty-day loan for a $15 deposit).

- Ask the **New England Anti-Vivisection Society (NEAVS),** 333 Washington St., Suite 850, Boston, MA 02108-5100, for addresses of companies that have programs, models, and films.

- Contact **Student Action Corp for Animals (SACA),** Box 15588, Washington, DC 20003-0588, for information on dissection and the humane alternatives and for information on forming a student group to protest dissection or other animal abuses.

Remember, *no one* should force you to hurt or kill an animal. Others may not seem to understand, but with the facts and the alternatives, they will learn from your determination and compassion.

45 STEP UP ON YOUR SOAPBOX

Your teacher wants you to give a speech in front of the class. You tell your classmates:

A. How to make a necklace out of bubblegum wrappers.
B. That "orangutan" means "person of the forest"—and how neat and gentle great apes are!

If your answer is B, you're *our* kind of animal!

DID YOU KNOW?

- If the idea of giving a speech makes you feel like the embarrassed zebra who was black and white and red all over, you're not alone—surveys have shown that speaking in public is the number one fear in America!
- Even Abraham Lincoln, a great speaker, probably had knocking knees and sweaty palms the first few times he stood up in front of people. Practice makes perfect: give lots of speeches and you'll

get used to standing up there in front of the class—or a whole assembly! You'll also give lots of people something to think about.

● Tiffany Wade, age thirteen, gave a five-minute speech during the March for the Animals in Washington, D.C., in front of more than twenty-five thousand people. Suddenly, a five-minute speech in front of a class of just twenty-five students doesn't seem so bad, does it?

● PETA Vegetarian Campaign Coordinator Robin Walker gave a speech to fifty-eight seventh-graders about factory farming and vegetarianism. Two weeks later, twenty-one members of the group had contacted her to find out more about dropping meat from their diet.

● Many humane societies have programs that include sending speakers to schools to discuss everything from humane treatment of companion animals to habitat destruction. A woman named Debbie Duel discovered that the humane society where she volunteered didn't have a humane education program. Thanks to Debbie, the Washington Humane Society now has a program in which Debbie talks to hundreds of students every year about the importance of respecting animals. One student who heard her speak said, a year later, "I used to hurt cats; now I help cats."

● Adam Locke, a high school student in California, arranged with a local TV station to tape a "Speak Out" message about a student's right to refuse to dissect animals. It didn't cost Adam a dime and was played on five different TV channels and a radio station!

WHAT YOU CAN DO

● If you are going to give a speech, here are some tips:

 • Choose one animal rights issue such as cosmetics testing, carriage horses, or the factory farming of chickens. It's hard to cover in five minutes all aspects of even one animal abuse issue and the many reasons why animals need to be protected.
 • Be sure your speech has a beginning, a middle, and an end.
 • Keep your sentences short and simple. You don't want to bore your audience—if they doze off, it will be hard to convince them of anything.

• Include specific examples: mention companies that still use animal tests (L'Oreal, for example), or show photographs of animals who got tangled in plastic trash. Members of your audience may otherwise have a hard time believing the problem.
• Tell listeners what they can do to help. If you talk about how animals are treated on farms, hand out tasty vegetarian recipes. If you discuss cosmetics testing, pass out lists of cruelty-free companies so your audience can get involved. The animals won't gain any friends if people don't know how to help.
• Practice makes perfect. Ask your family or a friend to listen to your speech, but don't rehearse *too* much or you'll sound like a computer.

• Talk to your teachers about getting a representative from a humane society or animal protection organization to speak to your class or school.
• Attend speeches given by other people. You may pick up tips you can use, and you'll have a chance to bring up your favorite subject at question time.
• Call or write the managers of your local radio and television stations to see if the station will let you tape a "Speak Out" on an animal issue.

CHECK IT OUT

• Call your local humane society to find out if they have a humane educator. Ask your teacher to get a speaker (or a film) for your school assembly.
• Contact **PETA,** P.O. Box 42516, Washington, DC 20015, for information on your topic. Write as soon as your assignment is given to be sure that you receive materials in time to help you write your speech!
• Turn to *PETA News* or other animal rights magazines for photographs to pass out to your class or to create a display to accompany your talk.

46 LOST AND FOUND

One night a little cat named Moomin climbed out an open window and went to investigate a fascinating smell coming from the other side of the street. It was so late that the street was very quiet, and Moomin didn't realize she'd done something dangerous. When it began to rain, she scrunched up under a bush to keep dry.

The rain stopped when morning came, but by then the street was full of cars carrying people to work and school. Moomin heard her companions calling for her, but she was too scared of the traffic to cross back. Hungry and wet, she crept through the neighborhood, looking for another way back, but before she knew it, she was lost.

That night Moomin fell asleep under a porch, exhausted. The barks of strange dogs kept waking her, and she jumped a mile when she saw a raccoon family come out of the storm sewer to look for food. For the first time in her life she was cold and dirty and her stomach ached. All she could do was hope.

Moomin's story is true. Her guardians did find her, but only because they searched for twelve days and did everything you will read in this chapter. It takes love and persistence, but having your friend home safe and sound will be worth the work.

DID YOU KNOW?

- Dogs and cats can easily get lost, especially if a storm frightens them or rain causes them to lose the scent of the way back home.
- About two million dogs are stolen each year. Some thieves sell them to research laboratories or pit bull trainers or as "guard dogs." According to a detective who tracks lost dogs, some animals have even been kidnapped and held for ransom.
- Fewer animals are stolen in winter than in summer when days are longer and more animals are left outside longer.

WHAT YOU CAN DO

- The best thing to do is to help your companion not to get lost in the first place. Never leave animals alone in cars, tied in front of stores, or even in your own backyard, unless people you trust are watching out for them. Thieves look in these places and only need a few seconds to take an animal.
- Fix places in your fence where animals can squeeze through. Put up a "Please Close the Gate" sign.
- Cats can roam long distances, so keep them safe and sound inside your home or screened porch. If you feel they must go out, buy cat-safe harnesses and long leashes, and let them go out and enjoy the yard whenever you do.
- Make sure dogs and cats always wear easy-to-see identification. Attach an ID tag securely to the animal's collar, and have your companion tattooed.

   - An ID tag for cats or young puppies can be hooked to a collar made out of sewing elastic, which won't strangle the animal if caught on a hook or tree limb.
   - Sticky glow-in-the-dark tape can be put on the collar to make your friend more visible at night.

• Put a painless, permanent tattoo on the animal's thigh or stomach. For a tattooer close to you, contact:

National Dog Registry, Box 116, Woodstock, NY 12498; telephone 1-800-NDR-DOGS.

Tattoo-A-Pet, 1625 Emmons Ave., Suite 1H, Brooklyn, NY 11235; telephone 1-800-828-8667.

• Take several photos of your animal friend now. They should show any unusual markings, a face close-up, and the whole animal.
• If allowed in your community, post sturdy signs that tell thieves they will be seen, such as "STOP THIEF! OUR PETS ARE BEING WATCHED!"

● Write to **PETA,** P.O. Box 42516, Washington, DC 20015, for a fact sheet on companion animal theft.
● If an animal turns up missing, look everywhere, and look again every day. Here's how:

• Visit area animal shelters daily. Leave a description and photo at each one.
• Check the lost and found section of your newspapers.
• Tack up "LOST" posters on trees, telephone poles, and bulletin boards. Give the animal's name and description and your phone number. If possible, put up a current photo of him or her.
• Call local veterinarians.
• Ask mail carriers, neighbors, and construction workers in your area for their help. These people are out and about in places and at times that you aren't and may have seen—and can keep a lookout for—your companion.
• Call out to the animal at night when it's quiet, and you might hear even a faint reply.
• Look under houses, call and listen at openings to drainage ditches, and look up in trees. Cats can squeeze into very small places and get stuck.
• Spray-paint big, simple messages on scrap lumber and place these signs at intersections where drivers can't miss them. Keep it simple, like "BLACK DOG LOST, CALL 555-4566."

• Go door to door in your neighborhood with fliers.

• Contact all local laboratories and animal dealers. (Your local humane society or animal rights group should have a list of them.) The federal Animal Welfare Act allows you to go inside and look for a lost animal. If you have trouble, you should call the police and/or the humane society for help.

• Check with sanitation crews who remove dead animals from roads.

• If you've moved recently, do everything you're doing in your new area in your old neighborhood, too. Sometimes confused by a move, companion animals have traveled far to return to their old homes.

• Offer a reward on your signs and in your ads. If you have an answering machine, tape a message with a description of your lost friend. Be sure your recording says when someone will answer in person. Thieves don't leave phone numbers!

• If school is in session, ask at the office of all the local schools to post a notice on the bulletin board and make an announcement over the loudspeaker.

● Organize a "Theft Watch" team with other concerned kids.

• Keep a file of the animals in your neighborhood (where they live, their names, descriptions, and so on). Tell neighbors what you're doing and warn them of the dangers of leaving animals alone outside. Try to get a photo of each animal.

• Distribute ID tag order forms (available at most veterinary clinics and animal shelters).

• Watch for people sitting in trucks and vans, especially those with out-of-state license plates. Write down the tag numbers and state, a description of the vehicle, and the date, time, and place it was seen. If you see an animal being stolen, notify the police at once.

47 | IT'S YOUR TURN TO SET THE TABLE

Question: What has four legs, goes to the mall, and spreads the word about animal rights?
Answer: Your animal rights information table!

DID YOU KNOW?

- You can have a great time at the mall without spending a nickel. Malls aren't just for shopping or hanging out anymore—they're for animal rights activities.
- You can introduce tons of people to animal rights issues at fairs and festivals in your town.
- You can fill petitions with hundreds of signatures in just a few hours at concerts, college student unions, malls, fairs, or any other place where lots of people will see you.
- You can help inform others without speaking a word. How? By setting up a table display at your library.

WHAT YOU CAN DO

● Plan early.

   • If you want to set up an animal rights information table at a fair
   or festival, make sure to call the mayor's office or the police station
   to see if you need permission and if there are any rules you need
   to follow. You might have to fill out a form, and it could take a
   few weeks to get approval.
   • To table at a mall, you simply need permission from the mall
   manager (to avoid problems later, get it in writing).
   • If you want to table outside a concert, call the local police
   department to find out if you need a permit. The streets in front
   of most concert halls are public property, so it's usually easy to
   get permission to table there.
   • If you'd rather be tabling inside the concert, contact the concert
   promoter listed on promotional posters and ads. A local radio
   station that is advertising the concert can also put you in contact
   with the promoter and might be willing to help you get the permission you need.

● Check with the librarian at your school's library or at your town's
   public library—you may be able to display information for several
   weeks!

● You'll need to get supplies and information.

   • If you don't have a card table, borrow one from a neighbor or
   look for one at flea markets or thrift stores in your area. Cover it
   with a clean sheet.
   • You can make posters with photographs and information clipped
   out of animal rights newsletters and glued onto posterboard. Posterboard can be found in almost any drugstore or art supply shop.
   • It's easy to make a donation can to keep on your table. Just use
   a clean, empty can. Cut a money slot into a plastic lid. You can
   make a label by wrapping paper around the can and decorating it

with animal rights messages, your group's name—anything. If you're collecting money for a specific organization, say so.
• You can make petitions to have people sign. At the top, write a simple description of what the petition is about—a local event, such as pig wrestling, or a business, such as horse-drawn carriages. Then draw lines across the rest of the page for people to sign their names, addresses, and signatures. Your petition should look something like this:

WE, the undersigned, ask the county government to ban pig wrestling from the county fair and other events held in our county:

NAME   ADDRESS   SIGNATURE
_____
_____
_____

• Once the petition is full of signatures, present it to the county council. Call the City Hall to find out who the council chairperson is and how you can make an appointment to meet with her or him. You can tell the local newspaper what you're doing and they might want to interview you about the problem.

● Mind your manners.

• Flash a smile—people who pass your table will feel more comfortable about coming up to you for information.
• Don't slouch—stand up! No one will be interested in your information if you're slumped over on a chair. They'll think it put even *you* to sleep!
• If you have friends helping you, zip your lips! Of course you can talk to each other, but don't ignore people who visit your table. They might be very interested and have important questions they need you to answer.
• Don't argue with rude people. Offer to give them information to take with them. If you spend too much time talking to someone who doesn't care, you might miss a chance to talk to someone who does!

- You'll be surprised how eager people are to learn how they can help animals. But don't be discouraged if a few people are unfriendly. Some people don't want to care about animals because they may have to make changes in their lives. Concern for animals is growing, and one day even those people will probably understand and agree.

CHECK IT OUT

- Write to **PETA,** P.O. Box 42516, Washington, DC 20015, for information on obtaining leaflets and petitions to use and display at your table. PETA can also send you a label for your donation can and posters to use at your table.

FIRST KID: "Heard you're taking a mountain climbing class this summer."

SECOND KID: "Yes. My mother says I've got to bring my grades up above C level!"

Some kids learn as much during their summer vacations as they do when they're in school. Somehow, learning is a lot more fun—and easy—when you're studying something you really like. You can use some of your vacation time to learn about animals and their habitats. When school's back in session, don't be shy about sharing your new knowledge and skills with your classmates!

DID YOU KNOW?

- There are lots of things you can do during the summer that benefit animals, even if you're vacationing.
- Cutting back on the amount of meat you eat is one way to help other-than-human beings. Vacations are good times to explore new foods and try new recipes.
- If you're already a vegetarian, or are becoming one, you might want to meet other kids who don't eat animals and who won't make fun of you for eating barbecued tofu! Starting a club is one way to meet kids with your interests—or you can go to an overnight summer camp that serves only vegetarian food.
- Closer to home, you can participate in animal protection programs working alongside shelter staff, learning how to care for companion animals, and doing other animal-related activities.

WHAT YOU CAN DO

- Consider attending an overnight camp that supports vegetarianism.

  - **Legacy International** is an overnight camp that offers programs focusing on peace, tolerance, and compassion—and offers vegetarian food. For kids ages eight to ten, each session lasts one or two weeks and includes games, stories, group meetings, field trips, and special guests. Kids ages eleven to fourteen choose from eight electives including video, sports, theater, global issues, outdoor living skills, cross-cultural relations and creative writing. For more information, write to Legacy International, Route 4, Box 265, Bedford, VA 24523, or call (703) 297-5982.
  - In Canada, **Au Grand Bois** (French for "in the great woods") offers campers lots of games and outdoor activities and also only serves vegetarian food. Write to Au Grand Bois, Ladysmith, Quebec J0X 2A0, Canada.

- If you live in Massachusetts, you can participate in the **Massachusetts Society for the Prevention of Cruelty to Animals** state-wide summer programs for children ages eight to thirteen. Sessions take place at various MSPCA shelters throughout the state and last one to two weeks. Kids work alongside MSPCA shelter staff caring for shelter animals, explore important animal protection issues, learn firsthand about responsible companion animal care, and discover how we share the Earth with wildlife. The cost is minimal, and there is a discount for MSPCA members. Some scholarships are available. For children in grades one through six, the Boston MSPCA also offers one-day sessions during the February and April school vacation weeks. For more information, including exact dates and fees, write to the MSPCA's Humane Education Department at 350 South Huntington Ave., Boston, MA 02130, or call (617) 541-5094.

- The **Animal Rescue League of Boston** offers a day camp program during the summer at its Animal Friends Summer School in Cataumet, Massachusetts. There are many activities to choose from, including care of small companion animals, dog training, environmental discovery, and nature crafts. A three-week session costs $165, a four-week session costs $220, and there are discounts when more than one child from a family attends. For more information, call or write Ed Powers, Director, Animal Rescue League of Boston, P.O. Box 265, Boston, MA 02117; (617) 426-9170.

- The **St. Louis Humane Society's Critters Camp,** for kids ages seven to twelve, teaches humane treatment of animals and lasts one week. Write or call Critters Camp, St. Louis Humane Society, 1210 Macklind Rd., St. Louis, MO 63110; (314) 647-8800.

- The **Peninsula Humane Society** in San Mateo, California, offers a program for kids ages nine to twelve, who take a three-hour class once a week for six weeks. Terms run year-round, not just in the summer. Kids learn about animal shelter operations, wildlife, endangered species, marine animals, and animal rights through slides, videos, and field trips. The course costs $35. Write Donna Smith at the Peninsula Humane Society, 12 Airport Blvd., San Mateo, CA 94401; (415) 340-7022, extension 344.

- The **San Francisco Society for the Prevention of Cruelty to Animals** offers a Middle School Career Exploration Week. In 1990 it was held in August, but it may now be offered in the spring and summer. In each session eight students research one of several careers, including veterinarian, shelter animals attendant, animal behaviorist, and animal control officer, and then prepare a display showing what they have learned. Students must submit applications describing their interest in the program, provide a teacher's recommendation, and have an interview at the SPCA. For more information, write to the San Francisco SPCA, 2500 16th St., San Francisco, CA 94103, or call (415) 554-3060.

• The **Marin Humane Society** has five sessions of summer camp for kids ages six to fifteen. The sessions last one to two weeks and cost $25 a week (includes a T-shirt). Campers enjoy activities such as learning basic care of companion animals, arts and crafts, and working in a shelter or barn. For details, write to the Education Department, Marin Humane Society, 171 Bel Marin Keys Blvd., Novato, CA 94949, or call (415) 883-4621.

• The **Progressive Animal Welfare Society** is developing after-school and summer programs for kids. Topics will include companion animal care, wildlife, and starting a club. For more information, write to the Education Coordinator at PAWS, P.O. Box 1037, Lynnwood, WA 98036, or call (206) 742-4142.

CHECK IT OUT

• Call or write your local humane society, animal shelter, or animal rights group to find out about animal protection programs and camps for kids in your area.

• Start a club! Summer vacation is the perfect time to get a bunch of kids together to form a group for animals. For ideas, see chapter 53, "Join the Club."

• Call, write, or drop into your local shelter to find out what you can do to help. The staff might be eager to have you walk the dogs, play with the cats, clean cages, fill water bowls, and the like. You can usually help out by collecting materials shelters never seem to have enough of—such as blankets, towels, sheets, newspapers, and leashes.

- Remember that all the information on programs in this chapter is likely to change at least a little bit over time. Be sure to contact the programs for more details and up-to-date information.

49 DEVELOP A GOOD ROADSIDE MANNER

When walking home from school, you see a robin looking dazed at the side of the road. You're in a hurry because there's a party that evening. You:

A. Keep going so you won't be late for the party.
B. Run home and ask your sister to go back and rescue the bird.
C. Stop, rescue the bird, and find a way to get the bird to a wildlife rehabilitator.

Letter C, of course. Little kindnesses matter all by themselves. When you fall and hurt yourself, it would be awful if people thought themselves too busy to stop and help. It's important to take time for anyone who is in trouble, no matter where you are going or how rushed you are.

DID YOU KNOW?

- Dogs and cats are sometimes abandoned along the road or at highway rest areas by people who imagine the animals will somehow learn to fend for themselves.

  - Eva-Jean Fridh of Georgetown, Texas, saw a dog alone at a rest area early one summer. She didn't stop because she thought surely the dog was just waiting for someone to come out of the restroom. Many weeks later, Eva-Jean and her family by chance ended up at the same rest area—only to find the same dog there! The dog was weak with hunger and thirst, was bitten all over by fire ants, and couldn't even stand up. Eva-Jean knew what she had to do. She brought the dog home, nursed her back to health, and named her Sandy. Sandy is full of energy today. Her coat is soft and shiny and her eyes sparkle with joy. Eva-Jean and her family saved Sandy's life, and now Sandy makes *their* lives even happier!

- Sometimes animals who have been hit on the highway are not dead, but unconscious or unable to get up and move away. It's always best to check if you have any doubt. Ask your parents to stop and when it's safe walk back with you to check on and care for an injured animal.

WHAT YOU CAN DO

- If you see a dog or cat running along the side of the road or hanging around a fast-food place or rest area, call Information for the local humane society's phone number and report the situation. Check back later to see if the animal is still there. If the animal is in danger of being hit by a car or picked up by a person with bad intentions, try to get him or her to come to you by using kind words and perhaps some food, and then take the animal home or to the local animal shelter.

● Someone could be looking for their pal, so put up simple "FOUND" signs on telephone polls, on bulletin boards, and in other public places. Give your phone number, but don't describe the animal in detail. You can only be certain the people who call you are the animal's true guardians if they can describe their companion completely.

● Stock your family's car with an animal rescue kit: a medium-size box with air holes punched in it, a blanket, some thick gloves, the phone numbers and addresses of veterinarians and wildlife rehabilitators, and a leash.

● Call around to find out which veterinarians will treat lost, injured animals for free and which will require that you pay. You may want to have a fund-raiser or gather donations so that you or the treasurer of your Neighborhood Animal Watch group (see chapter 15) will have funds on hand to take care of a stray animal emergency.

● Birds are often stunned by cars. Any birds found on or at the side of the road should be picked up *very gently*, put into a box with air holes punched in it or a paper sack with the top folded over, then taken to a wildlife rehabilitator. Birds are terrified of people, so don't let anyone hold them, pet them, or make a lot of noise, and don't stare at them.

● When you see animals lying at the side of the road, always take the time to stop and check whether they're still alive. You should do this without touching the animals, because that might startle or hurt them more. If you aren't sure if they're still breathing, here's how to check:

• First, of course, make absolutely sure *you* are in no danger from traffic. Get a grownup to help you remove the animal, using gloves or a towel, to the safety of the curb, away from the pavement.

• You may be able to see light breathing by looking at an animal's chest. If not, take a twig or a piece of rolled-up newspaper and, very gently, touch the animal's eye. If there is any movement, she or he is alive. If not, you have helped anyway, because crows, possums, and other animals who clean the Earth by surviving on carcasses won't be killed while eating.

- If you can tell that the animal in the road is alive but badly hurt, flag down a police officer or call the humane society. Ask people to help get the animal to the side of the road gently and carefully. Animals who are hurt and scared can bite in self-defense. Try to have someone stay with the animal at all times.

- If you find a female opossum you know is dead, call a wildlife rehabilitator and ask them to check to see if she has a pouch full of babies. Since opossums carry their babies in stomach pouches, the babies may not have been hurt in the accident. If you find babies, keep them all together in a small box with air holes punched in it and on a soft towel, and call the nearest wildlife rehabilitator as soon as possible. These babies need very special care that only a wildlife rehabilitator can give them (contact the local humane society or animal control office for the name of a wildlife rehabilitator).

- The best thing to do is prevent animals from being hit by cars in the first place. Here are some ideas:

  - Get your class to write letters to the mayor asking that barriers such as concrete slabs be put up along local roads and highways where you see a lot of animals hurt. (Your local library has the mayor's name and address.)
  - Encourage your city officials to help prevent cars from hitting animals by keeping grass, shrubs, and trees cut back from the roadside at least several feet. When plants are put right next to the road, they attract animals who eat them or are looking for places to live.
  - And, of course, do not let "companimals" outside without a leash unless they're in a fenced-in yard (dogs) or a screened-in porch (cats).

CHECK IT OUT

- Write to **Friends of Animals,** P.O. Box 1244, Norwalk, CT 06856, for a bumper sticker that reads "Caution: I Brake for Animals" ($1) to put on your family's car.

- Order some free brochures to distribute that explain why dogs and cats should be kept indoors unless supervised. Write to **PETA**, P.O. Box 42516, Washington, DC 20015.
- For more information about wildlife rehabilitation and to find a rehab center or certified "rehabber" near you, contact the following organizations. Write them *before* an emergency comes up, so you'll be prepared.

• **International Wildlife Rehabilitation Council (IWRC)**, 4437 Central Pl., Suite B4, Suisan, CA 94585.
• **National Wildlife Rehabilitation Association (NWRA)**, 708 Riverside Ave. So., Sartrell, MN 56377.

- Here's a short list of regional wildlife rehabilitation centers you can turn to for help:

HOWL, the PAWS Wildlife Center
Box 1037
Lynnwood, WA 98046
(206) 743-1884

Peninsula Humane Society Wildlife Center
12 Airport Blvd.
San Mateo, CA 94401
(415) 573-3720

Wildlife Rescue Inc.
Box 15223
Austin, TX 78781-5223
(512) 836-0915

University of Minnesota Wildlife Rehabilitation Clinic
St. Paul, MN 55108
(612) 624-7730

Wild Animal Rehabilitation Center
5800 North Lovers Lane Road
Milwaukee, WI 53225
(414) 358-0144

Willowbrook Wildlife Haven
525 S. Park Blvd.
Glen Ellyn, IL 60137

Wildlife Center of Virginia
Box 98
Weyers Cave, VA 24486
(703) 234-9453

Chesapeake Wildlife Sanctuary
17308 Queen Anne Bridge Road
Bowie, MD 20716
(301) 390-7010

Suncoast Seabird Sanctuary
18328 Gulf Boulevard
Indian Shores, FL 33535
(813) 391-6211

Wildlife Rescue Association, B.C.
5216 Glencarin Drive
Burnaby, B.C.   V5B 3C1
CANADA

50 ADD A LITTLE SPICE TO THEIR LIVES

Who likes pasta, garbanzo beans, peas, corn, fruit, and rice?

A. Dogs.
B. Cats.
C. People.
D. All of the above.

Letter D is correct! We all like variety in our diets. In fact, dogs even like garlic. (But does that make their bark worse than their bite?)

In the jungles of the Gombe in Tanzania, Africa, members of chimpanzee families spend many hours each day gathering food. In one month they can collect and eat as many as forty to sixty different kinds of leaves, roots, fruits, and seeds from trees with names like Ipomoea, Dalbergia, and Harungana. Some foods taste very sweet, while others are quite bitter. Some things these great apes chew on are natural medicines—chimpanzees, like many tribal humans, seem always to have known how to find and pick natural, herbal remedies to treat their illnesses and injuries.

DID YOU KNOW?

- Just like the chimpanzees, dogs in the wild, whether dingoes of Australia, pariah dogs of Asia, or wolves and foxes in the Americas, eat a very varied diet. Just like people, all dogs may fancy a particular taste one day and something different the next.
- Canids (that's the dog family name) are taught by their mothers to select many varieties of wild berries and to hunt for small creatures. But, like captive chimpanzees who can't get out of the zoo or the laboratory, dogs and cats and other animals who live with humans have no choice; they eat what they're given day after day. Many dogs and cats kept in human households eat just one kind of food—often some sort of boring canned glop or dry pellets—for their whole lives. That's pretty dull!
- Of course, letting companion animals outdoors in our busy, built-up world wouldn't work. Not only are there precious few of the right kind of berry bushes for them to feed on and wild creatures to hunt, but no one taught them as youngsters that those kinds of things are edible. Our friends would probably starve.
- Never fear, you can help. Pep up your cat's or dog's (or even hamster's) diet by baking or "foraging" for them.

WHAT YOU CAN DO

- Please them with pasta! You'd think most dogs come from Italy because they really love spaghetti (with a little tomato sauce) and other noodle dishes. Fresh garlic is not only good for dogs (it's a blood cleanser and flea and tick repellent), but sprinkled on food, it can be a big hit with the canine crowd. Like pasta, rice is not only good for dogs, but most of them enjoy it as long as it is mixed with something tasty (like noodles, bread, or kibble).
- Mix it up. Gravies, especially brown gravies, and even barbecue sauces are often a big hit with dogs and cats. Mashed cooked carrots, cooled down, and nutritional yeast get rave reviews from some other-than-humans.

- Cut up in the kitchen! Fresh-cut carrots (raw, this time) and chunks of washed apple or pear are liked not only by dogs who like to crunch, but also by hamsters, mice, rats, rabbits, and gerbils. Unsalted nuts are also usually gladly received. Try giving them in the shell. If cracking the shell seems too tough for your friend, shelled unsalted nuts do just fine. Best of all, some rodents like to eat wild flowers, like clover and dandelions.
- Be a chef for a *chat* (that's French for "cat"). Cats' tastes vary a lot. Some cats like melon, others like rye bread pieces (a whole slice is usually too hard to manage), and lentil soup or soy milk are favorites of others.
- Tempt them with tofu. Lots of dogs and cats enjoy bean curd mashed up with gravy or mixed with other foods.
- Here are two easy-to-fix recipes created specially for dogs and cats:

DOG BISCUITS (PETA recipe collection)

4½ c. whole-wheat flour
½ c. nutritional yeast (check your local health food store)
½ tbsp. salt
½ tbsp. garlic powder

Mix dry ingredients. Add about 1½ cups water. Knead into a big ball of dough. Roll dough out with a rolling pin on a piece of wax paper until it is a big flat circle. Cut into shapes with your favorite cookie cutters. Put dog "cookies" on a cookie sheet and bake for 10–15 minutes with the oven set at 350° F. After all the biscuits are baked, leave them in the oven overnight so they get hard and crunchy.

GARBANZO CAT CHOW (courtesy Harbingers of a New Age— see address on page 205)

⅜ c. cooked garbanzo beans (also called chick-peas—you can buy them already cooked in a can at the grocery store)
1½ tbsps. nutritional yeast powder
1 tbsp. chopped or grated vegetables (lots of cats especially love corn!)

1 tbsp. oil
½ tsp. Vegecat supplement (ordering information at end of chapter)
⅓ tsp. soy sauce

Mix all the ingredients together and serve warm. They love it!

● Follow these feeding tips:

• Feed companion animals *before* you and your family eat. When they have to wait until afterward, dogs can get worried they've been forgotten and start asking for food during your meal.
• When you've finished feeding, always say, "All gone," and give an upturned palms ("empty hands") signal, followed by a scratch behind the ears (theirs, not yours!)

CHECK IT OUT

● You can order nutritional supplements for your dogs and cats from **Harbingers of a New Age,** 12100 Brighton St., Hayden Lake, ID 83835. Each order comes with a bunch of free recipes! If you want your cats to become vegetarian, you *must* include the Vegecat nutritional supplement in their food *every day*. As true carnivores (meat eaters), cats have special nutritional requirements that are tricky, but not impossible, to meet on a vegetarian diet.

51 | MAKE SURE FAIR IS FAIR

One little piggy was prodded and raced
Another little piggy was greased and chased
Yet a third little piggy was thrown to the ground
So this little piggy
Complained all around!

—**JONATHAN CANBY,** age eight

DID YOU KNOW?

● At some fairs, "diving" mules climb a rickety ramp to a thirty-foot-high platform and then plunge into the water going thirty miles an hour. If you've ever done a belly flop from the high diving board, you know how bad it must feel! Even water buffalo, who love a good soaking, wouldn't *dive* into the river. Large animals have to shift their weight carefully so they don't hurt themselves.

- Have you heard the dirty joke about the pig who wallowed in the mud? Pigs really are clean—they only lie in the mud when they need to cool off. But people at fairs sometimes cover them with grease and wrestle them. Most people would say that yanking on the ears and tails of dogs and tackling them to the ground is cruel; why shouldn't this go for pigs, too?

- Many "wrestling" bears and alligators have their teeth and claws removed so they can't hurt people who try to pin them down. Needless to say, those bears would rather be in the woods—and the alligators back in the swamps—than in cramped, hot cages.

- Did you hear about the turtle who stopped racing the rabbit because he always lost by a hare? That might sound funny, but making animals race is really no laughing matter! Imagine being packed into an un-air-conditioned truck and shipped all over the country— and only being taken out of your cage to be prodded around a racetrack in the scorching heat.

- All kinds of animals are raced—including ducks, frogs, llamas, turtles, slugs, pigs, ostriches, turkeys, and crabs. Certainly animals who are raced would keep on running (or waddling or crawling or hopping) after they crossed the finish line, if they could!

- Dancing chickens don't really know how to tango—they are shocked into jumping around by jolts of electricity sent through wires in the floor.

- Ponies at carousel rides work long hours, walking around and around in the hot sun. There are no Gatorade breaks for carousel ponies—they're lucky if they even get a sip of water.

- Baby animals used in petting zoos are lonely, sad animals bought from breeders who take them from their mothers before they are ready to be on their own. Just like human babies, lion and bear cubs rely on their mothers until they are grown up.

- Animals used in petting zoos and wrestling acts often wind up on hunting ranches (where people pay to "bag a trophy") when they get old. Pigs who are wrestled or raced wind up as the main course at barbecues as soon as they get too big and their track days are over.

- On a lighter note, **Great American Duck Races,** a Phoenix, Arizona, company, rents out rubber ducks for charity fund-raiser races. Organizers rent the racing ducks and then round up sponsors to adopt the birds, usually for $5 a duck—offering prizes for the winners. In a lake or pond, people can keep track of and collect back all of the ducks, so it's loads of fun. However, we don't recommend "duck" races on a river because they could float to the ocean and be swallowed by sea animals.

WHAT YOU CAN DO

- Steer clear of acts or events that use animals. If no one goes to petting zoos, animal wrestling events, or exhibits where chickens in little boxes dance and caged rabbits play the piano, people won't make money from these events. They'll find ways to make money without causing animals to suffer.
- Ask people to think about what happens to "show animals." When they realize what the animals go through, people will think twice about attending such events.
- Complain to managers who book animal acts. Let them know that these events are no fun for animals: ponies don't enjoy going in circles for hours, and "diving" mules remember the fear and abuse they endured in order to learn to dive. Animals just want to be left in peace.
- Set up a face painting booth at the county fair. As you paint whiskers and/or kind messages on fair-goers' faces, hand out literature that informs about the mistreatment of animals.

CHECK IT OUT

- Contact **PETA,** P.O. Box 42516, Washington, DC 20015, for free fact sheets and leaflets about animal shows. You can copy the information to give to your family and friends or to hand out at a demonstration.
- If your town fair is planning animal races, contact the organizers and tell them the facts. If animals wanted to be sports celebrities, they'd organize their own Olympics! Suggest human "crab," wheelbarrow, or gunnysack races instead.
- People can have fun creating paper origami (pronounced "or-ee-gahm-ee") frogs. Check out books on how to create origami an-

imals at your local library and bookstores. You and your friends will keep busy for hours creating all sorts of paper animals in this ancient Japanese art form.

● If you see animals performing, check for the following:

• Do the animals have plenty of clean water? Are their cages and pens clean?
• Can they stand up, sit down, and turn around comfortably? Do they have shade and shelter?
• Do they look healthy, or are they sick, tired, or thirsty? Are their coats shiny (a sign of good health)? Or do they have any open cuts, sores, or scars?

● It can be helpful if you can take photographs of any animals who look sick or abused. Send the information to animal protection groups that can improve the conditions for the animals—maybe even get them retired to a sanctuary or some other friendly place.

52 | GET POETIC

Billy Shakespeare

Only you are you,
Said the wise old gnu,
So do your special miracles
That no one else can do.
—**BECKY MORGANTHALER,**
age eleven

For poetry ideas sure to be treasured, not trashed, look to other-than-human beings for inspiration. We all have creative talents, whether or not we are aware of them and whether or not we develop them. Expressing your feelings creatively is fun and can influence other people's feelings about animals. And feelings are some of the most powerful forces on Earth!

DID YOU KNOW?

- Some people are at their creative best in the morning.
- Others' creativity blossoms at night.

● It's handy to have paper and pen near your bed, in case you awaken in the night with a good idea.

WHAT YOU CAN DO

Here are some projects and examples, many of which were suggested by Donna Smith of the Peninsula Humane Society in *Critters and Kids Chronicle,* Spring 1990 (for ordering information, write to Peninsula Humane Society, 12 Airport Blvd., San Mateo, CA 94401).

● Write a paper or story from a wolf's or other animal's point of view. If we could understand other animals' languages, what would we hear? If you were a cat, or a dog, or some other-than-human animal, what would you say about:

- why you love a certain human—or kids in general?
- what it's like to be hunted?
- what you would do if you could escape from your cage or get unchained?
- having fun playing together as a school of fish?
- why not to go near people?
- exploring the ocean as a young whale?
- leaving the nest and learning to fly?

● Try your hand at "subject," "tanka," "haiku," and "cinquain" poems.

- Write a subject poem (sometimes called an "acrostic") by placing the letters of the subject in a column. Then write a line about the subject for each letter. For example:

> Wonderful
> Outcast
> Loyal to each other
> Feared

- Tanka poems have five lines with five syllables in the first and third lines and seven syllables each in the second, fourth, and fifth lines. Here's one about a fish:

Yellow and white stripes
undulating through rolling
warm azure ocean,
her eyes wide, sheer tail steering
flawless innocence through life.

• Haiku poems were first written in Japan. They have three lines
and the syllable pattern 5-7-5. *Choices: The Farm and You* (The
Athene Trust, 1989) printed this poem, which the haiku poet Issa
wrote about two hundred years ago:

Snail, my little man,
Slowly!—oh very slowly—
Climb up Fujisan!

• Cinquain poems are five-line, unrhymed poems that are fun and
easy to write. A cinquain can show an animal to be complete and
important for his or her own sake, so it's a good way to write
nicely about an animal many people dislike or fear. Use these
guidelines from *Choices*:

Rat
1 noun (animal's name or title)

Curious   friend
2 words describing the animal

Never   hurt   anyone
3 words expanding the idea

Wants   to   be   happy
4 words describing how you feel about this animal

Misunderstood
1 word to sum up the poem

CHECK IT OUT

• Put your pen to paper and try a poem about an animal most people
think is scary or ugly or silly or dirty. Let people know all animals
are special!

53 | JOIN THE CLUB

Unscramble the words to find out what people in animal rights clubs do (answers are at the end of the chapter):

1. ewitr sitelte (two words)
2. lebat
3. felatle
4. tedbae
5. tcipek

DID YOU KNOW?

- By starting an animal rights club, you can help animals, make new friends, and have a whale of a time!
- Two heads are better than one, and three are even better. Let others know you're helping animals and they'll want to get involved, too.
- Ryan Shumate and Jennifer Kolb started their own animal rights club in Virginia called Prevention of Cruelty to Animals (POCTA).

Ryan and Jennifer make their own quarterly newsletter on a computer, covering topics ranging from fur to zoos. They even include a vegetarian dining column full of recipes. Their activities, including leafleting and regularly calling 800 numbers (see chapter 22), were covered in a two-page article in a local newspaper!

● Students at Franconia Elementary School held a contest to see who could collect the most supplies for the Wildlife Rescue League in Falls Church, Virginia, which helps injured and orphaned animals.

WHAT YOU CAN DO

● Organize a few friends who are interested in helping animals. If you get busy, others will want to join.

• Decide whether your group wants to focus your efforts on a single issue, such as carriage horses or fur, or lots of different animal issues.
• When your group has decided what to work on, pick a name that describes what your club is about, such as Animal Allies, Veggie Kids, or Friends of Carriage Horses. Then choose a motto like "Just say 'no' to animal cruelty" or "Eat beans, not beings" or "Animals are not ours to eat, wear, or experiment on."

● Set up literature tables to inform others, protest cruel activities, and gather names on petitions. (See chapter 47 for ideas.)
● Set up a booth at your school's fair and paint whiskers, animal faces, and/or kind messages on people who stop by. Maybe you'll find new club members!
● The Marin Humane Society of Novato, California, suggests making an inexpensive banner with a twin-size sheet and markers or textile (fabric) paint (art stores usually have the right kind of markers and paint). Spread out the banner on top of newspapers (so you don't stain the floor) and make sure that there are no wrinkles. Print your animal rights message and, if you like, draw a picture of an animal. Use the banner to recruit new members at a school club fair, at demonstrations (you may need to cut slits in it if it's windy so it doesn't act like a sail), at fund-raisers for your group, or anywhere you want to stand up and be noticed.

- Hold letter-writing parties (see chapter 29). Serve vegetarian food like apples and peanut butter, hummus and pita bread, or whatever your favorite is.
- Do some fund-raising.

• To raise funds for your club, scrub a Bug (or a Cougar, Fox, or Rabbit!) at a weekend car wash. Or have a vegan bake sale, clean up your room and hold a garage sale, or announce a "favorite animal friend" photo contest at school. Contest entry fees of $.50 or $1 can all go to help the club.

• Promote your fund-raiser by making and distributing fliers (make them simple, clear, and eye-catching so people will read them); putting up posters at the supermarket, school, churches, and other community spots (with permission); spreading the news "word of mouth"; and possibly taking out ads in your school and local newspapers.

• Once you have the money, you can buy art supplies, memberships to organizations, subscriptions to magazines, stamps, paper and envelopes for mailings, and whatever else your club might need. You might consider donating what's left over to an animal protection group or local shelter.

CHECK IT OUT

- Call PETA's tape-recorded **Action Line** every week to find out what's going on: (301) 770-8980. If it's not a local call, phone at night or on the weekend to save money, with permission from your parents. Write to **PETA,** P.O. Box 42516, Washington, DC 20015, for more ideas, free fliers, and to subscribe to *PETA Kids* magazine ($3 a year).
- Join **The Kindness Club,** 65 Brunswick St., Fredericton, N.B., E3B 165, Canada. For $3, The Kindness Club members receive a packet of information, a membership card and pin, and a subscription to the club's bimonthly newsletter.
- Find out what ideas, materials, and support the organizations in appendix B have to offer your group.

Answers to word scramble:

1. write letters
2. table
3. leaflet
4. debate
5. picket

54 HANG IN THERE!

You've decided to stop eating animals, but your parents say you have to finish your dinner, including that hamburger. You:

A. sneak scraps to the dog when your parents aren't looking.
B. spit it into your napkin.
C. sulk and give your parents the silent treatment.

None of the above! Instead of sneaking, spitting, or sulking, ask them to listen to what you've learned about animals and why you want to help them. Adults can learn a lot from kids!

DID YOU KNOW?

- Sarah Hoeb of Ohio convinced her father to take veal off the menu at his Clarion Hotel restaurant after discussing the cruel treatment of calves.
- Megan Thompson of Texas was upset when her teacher told the class that branding doesn't hurt cattle. Megan's teacher didn't

217

understand her concern until she set up a meeting with Megan and her mother. They showed her articles and a videotape about how cattle are hurt when they are branded. The teacher was so moved by Megan's presentation that she joined Megan in a talk to the whole class about the cruelties of branding animals.

- Rhonda Mitchell of Oregon was upset when her grandmother gave her a rabbit fur coat for Christmas. Rhonda didn't want to hurt her grandmother's feelings, but she knew she couldn't accept the coat. After Rhonda told her the facts about fur, Rhonda's grandmother agreed to take the cruelty out of her closet, too. They delivered the rabbit fur jacket and an old fox fur coat to a nearby wildlife rehabilitator, who used the coats for orphaned animal babies to snuggle in!

- River Phoenix's whole family stopped eating meat and all animal products after River asked a few simple questions about eating animals. River says that he was about seven years old and on a boat with some friends who were fishing when he first became aware of cruelty to animals. He remembers, "Every time they caught a fish, they'd hurl it against a board that had nails sticking out of it. I couldn't believe it. These weren't bad people, but they'd become totally desensitized to the pain they were causing. My brother and I started asking my parents why we had to take animal lives to eat, and what exactly was in our hamburgers and hot dogs. Pretty soon my whole family decided it wasn't our place to block another creature's right of way, so we became vegetarians. But it took us kids to start asking the questions."

WHAT YOU CAN DO

- Don't get mad! Others might wonder why you care so much about animals and might not share your feelings about protecting them. Many people are taught to think of animals as nothing more than "things." But with patience and the facts, you can help them understand.

- Don't get discouraged! Some people might feel uncomfortable when you talk about respecting animals instead of using them. Some might even try to make fun of you. Let them know that animals should be thought of as friends and it's weird not to care about them. Tell them that what's best for any animal is best for *all* animals, including us.

- Don't give up! It might seem hard at times to make others understand why you refuse to cut up animals in biology class, why you won't wear animal skins, or why you don't want to eat your friends. People have used animals for food, clothing, and entertainment for centuries, but just because something is a tradition doesn't mean it's right. Remember, slavery was once an accepted tradition in the United States and other countries. It takes time to help people kick old habits.

- Think of people who have struggled (and won), or are still struggling, to gain their freedom and rights. When humans band together, they can make wonderfully positive changes. If we work together for animals (that is, *all* animals—other-than-human beings *and* people), we'll have a much better world.

CHECK IT OUT

- If you need information on activities to help animals and ideas on how to get others involved in animal protection, you can join **PETA Kids,** P.O. Box 42516, Washington, DC 20015, for $3. You will receive the newsletter twice a year and an action bulletin (*Brainstorm*) every other month—both will help you get the word out to others about animal rights. PETA Kids can also give you advice on how to help your friends and family understand your commitment to protecting animals.

- You can subscribe to *Otterwise,* a quarterly newsletter "for kids who love animals." Send your name, address, and $4 to **Otterwise,** P.O. Box 1374, Portland, ME 04104.

- Write for a free information pack from **Animal Aid Youth Group,** 7 Castle St., Tonbridge, Kent TN9 1BH, England. They offer lots of advice and support—mainly for British kids, ages twelve to eighteen—but would love to hear from you, too.

APPENDIX A:
Recipes for
Kids Who Care

Here's a handful of delicious, easy-to-make recipes:

YUMMY EGGLESS BANANA BREAD (1 loaf)
adapted from *I Love Animals and Broccoli,* by Debra Wasserman and
Charles Stahler (The Vegetarian Resource Group, P.O Box 1463, Baltimore, MD 21203; 1986)

½ c. margarine (1 stick)
4 *ripe* bananas
1¾ c. flour
½ tsp. baking soda
¼ c. soy milk or water

In a bowl, mash together bananas and the margarine with a fork. Add
flour, baking soda, and water. Mix well. Pour into oiled loaf pan. Bake
for one hour at 350° F.

SPANISH RICE
also from *I Love Animals and Broccoli*

1 onion, chopped
1 c. brown or white rice
2 c. water
2 green peppers, chopped
1 tbsp. chili powder
2 cloves garlic, chopped (or 1 Tbsp. garlic powder)
1 tbsp. soy sauce (optional)
2 tbsps. oil
2 tbsps. tomato paste

Cook above ingredients together covered, over medium heat until rice is soft—20–30 minutes for white, or 40–50 minutes for brown, rice (follow directions on package).

TOFU BURRITOS, by Dorothy R. Bates
Kids Can Cook (The Book Publishing Company, Summertown, TN 38483; 1987). Serves 10.

Mix together in a medium-size bowl:
1 tsp. flour
2 tsps. chili powder
1 tsp. cumin
1 tsp. salt
½ tsp. basil or oregano

When spices are mixed, crumble in finely and mix:
1 lb. firm tofu

Heat a heavy skillet over, and cook over, medium heat:
3 tbsps. oil and the seasoned tofu mix.
Fry for about five minutes, using a pancake turner to keep the mix from sticking to the pan as it heats.

Cook one at a time on a hot, dry griddle to barely brown both sides:
10 flour tortillas (check to see that there's no lard, and use whole wheat
if you can get them)
Put a big spoonful of filling on each one and serve rolled up with salsa
and chopped lettuce, onion, and tomato. If a cheese flavor is desired,
add a teaspoonful or so of nutritional yeast to the filling.

PIZZA SANDWICH
adapted from *The Cookbook for People Who Love Animals*, by Gentle
World (P.O. Box U, Paia, HI 96779)

1 slice whole-wheat bread
2 to 3 tomato slices
1 onion slice
1 tsp. sesame seeds
3 tbsps. nonmeat spaghetti sauce
1 tsp. nutritional yeast, for a cheesy flavor

Warm the bread in a toaster oven or under the broiler in your stove;
before it browns, remove it and spread with spaghetti sauce. Layer with
the tomato, the onion, sesame seeds, spaghetti sauce, and nutritional
yeast on top; place in the toaster oven or broiler, and toast for 3 to 4
minutes until golden brown.

STEAMED BABY CARROTS FOR TWO, by Robin Walker

16 baby carrots, scraped
1 tsp. margarine
⅛ tsp. ground nutmeg

Steam the baby carrots in a saucepan with just enough water to cover
the bottom for about 4 minutes. Drain and mix with the margarine and
nutmeg. Use 8 carrots for each serving and arrange them on plates in
a fan shape with the narrow tips pointing down.

BAKED TOFU LOAF
from the PETA recipe collection

1 medium onion, chopped fine
1c. whole-grain bread crumbs, rolled oats *or* cornflakes, crushed
1½ lbs. firm tofu, crumbled
½ cup fresh parsley, chopped
⅓ cup soy sauce
⅓ cup ketchup
2 tbsps. prepared mustard
¼ tsp. black pepper
¼ tsp. garlic powder

Preheat oven to 350° F. Mix all ingredients together. Put ¼ cup of oil in a loaf pan, then press the mixture into the pan. Bake for about 1 hour.

Let it cool 10–15 minutes before removing from pan. The loaf is great as part of a Thanksgiving meal and is also good sliced for sandwiches the next day.

PANCAKES, by Robin Walker

In a medium-size bowl, mix together the wet ingredients:
2 tbsps. oil
1⅓ c. water or ⅔ c. soy milk + ⅓ c. water

In a separate container, sift together the dry ingredients:
1¼ c. whole-wheat flour
2 tbsps. sugar (white or brown)
2 tsps. baking powder
½ tsp. salt

Make a hole in the center of the dry ingredients. Pour the wet ingredients into the dry and mix with a wooden spoon only until ingredients are blended. The batter should be a bit lumpy, which makes the pancakes light. (Smooth batter makes for tough cakes.)

Heat your griddle over medium high heat. It's hot enough when water dropped on it turns to beads and bounces across the pan. Then put 2 tbsps. oil or margarine on the griddle. Pour the batter into little puddles and flip cakes when little bubbles form on the top. Watch carefully to make sure they don't burn! Serves three people.

CHOCOLATE CHIP COOKIES, by Robin Walker

Preheat oven to 350° F.

Mix and set aside:
2¾ c. flour
1 tsp. salt
1 tsp. baking soda

Cream together:
1 c. margarine
¾ c. brown sugar
¾ c. sugar
1 tsp. vanilla
2 eggs' worth of egg replacer (**Ener-G Egg Replacer** is best—follow box directions). *Or,* mix 2 tsps. cornstarch with ¼ cup water and add to sugar mixture.

Add flour mixture to sugar mixture and mix well. Add 12 oz. dark chocolate chips and mix. Drop by spoonfuls onto a lightly oiled cookie sheet. Bake for 8–10 minutes. Yield: 40 cookies.

CHOCOLATE CUPCAKES, by Robin Walker

Preheat oven to 350° F.

In large bowl mix:
3 c. flour
2 c. sugar
6 tbsps. cocoa
2 tsps. baking soda

Make large crater in flour mixture and pour in, without mixing:
10 tbsps. melted margarine
2 tbsps. vinegar
2 tsps. vanilla

Next, pour 2 cups cold water over entire mixture and mix well. Pour mixture into oiled cupcake pans (or use paper cupcake holders instead of oil or margarine). Fill each cupcake ¾ full. Bake for 20 to 25 minutes or until a toothpick inserted in the center comes out clean. Yield: 26 cupcakes.

VANILLA FROSTING (for cupcakes)

Mix until creamy:
12 oz. powdered sugar
¾ c. margarine
⅛ c. vanilla soy milk

Consistency of frosting may vary. Add more sugar, margarine, or soy milk as needed.

SILKY CHOCOLATE PUDDING, by Robin Walker
PETA's Vegetarian Campaign Coordinator

This recipe uses a food processor, so you'll need the help of a parent. Otherwise, it's really quite easy.

6 oz. semisweet chocolate chips
2 10-oz. packages silken tofu
2 tbsps. brown sugar
¼ tsp. nutmeg
2 medium bananas, sliced

Melt the chocolate chips in a saucepan with one tablespoon of water. Combine melted chocolate and silken tofu in the container of a food processor and process until smooth. Add the brown sugar and nutmeg and process again until mixed well. Divide half the pudding among 6 dessert cups or small bowls and top with a layer of sliced bananas, followed by the remaining pudding. Chill for at least an hour before eating. Serve cold.

CHOCOLATE/PEANUT-BUTTER FUDGE

6 oz. (1 cup) semisweet chocolate chips
¼ c. brown sugar
2 tbsps. vanilla soy milk
½ c. oatmeal
⅓ c. natural peanut butter, at room temperature

Combine the chocolate, sugar, and soy milk in the top of a double boiler or in a small aluminum bowl set on top of a saucepan filled with two inches or so of water. Cook over low heat until smoothly melted. Stir in the oatmeal. Then drop in the peanut butter by teaspoonfuls. Swirl it in until evenly distributed but not blended in.

Line a small, shallow baking dish with wax paper. Put in the chocolate mixture with the help of a rubber spatula. Refrigerate for at least four hours until firm. Cut into 1-inch squares.

APPENDIX B:
Organizations and
Others for Animals

The following groups, magazines, and other folks were mentioned somewhere in this book. Here's how you can reach them. Remember, when you mail a letter overseas you need to put one air mail stamp or two regular stamps on the envelope and write "AIR MAIL" at the top. To send money overseas, find out which of your local banks can give you a foreign money order. Many banks will charge $5 to $10 to transfer your U.S. dollars into British pounds.

ORGANIZATIONS

- **African Wildlife Foundation:** 1717 Massachusetts Ave., N.W., Washington, DC 20036; 1-800-344-TUSK.
- **American Humane Association:** P.O. Box 1266, Denver, CO 80201-1266.
- **Animal Aid Youth Group:** 7 Castle St., Tonbridge, Kent TN9 1BH, England.

- **Animal and Environmental Defense Association:** P.O. Box 822, New Albany, IN 47150.
- **Animal Rescue League of Boston:** P.O. Box 265, Boston, MA 02117.
- **Animal Welfare Institute (AWI):** P.O. Box 3650, Washington, DC 20007.
- **Black Beauty Ranch:** P.O. Box 367, Murchison, TX 75778.
- **Campaign for the Abolition of Angling:** P.O. Box 14, Romsey SO51 9NN, England.
- **Center for Environmental Education:** 1725 DeSales St., N.W., Washington, DC 20036.
- **Chesapeake Wildlife Sanctuary:** 17308 Queen Anne Bridge Road, Bowie, MD 20716.
- **Chickens Lib:** P.O. Box 2, Holmsfirth, Huddersfield HD7 1QT, England.
- **The Children's Rainforest:** P.O. Box 936, Lewiston, ME 04240.
- **CHOICE!:** Parkdale, Dunham Rd., Altrincham, Cheshire WA14 4QG, England.
- **Coastal States Organization:** c/o Margie Fleming, 444 N. Capitol St., N.W., Suite 312, Washington, DC 20001.
- **Compassion in World Farming:** 20 Lavant St., Petersfield, Hampshire GU32 3EW, England.
- **The Cousteau Society:** 8440 Santa Monica Blvd., Los Angeles, CA 90069-4221.
- **Defenders of Wildlife:** 1244 19th St., N.W., Washington, DC 20036.
- **Dissection Hotline:** 1-800-922-FROG.
- **Division of Solid Waste Management:** Agency of Natural Resources, 103 S. Main St., West Building, Waterburg, VT 05676.
- **The Dolphin Project, Inc.:** P.O. Box 224, Coconut Grove, FL 33233.
- **Earth Island Institute:** 300 Broadway, Suite 28, San Francisco, CA 94133.
- **ELEFRIENDS:** Cherry Tree Cottage, Coldharbour Lane, Dorking, Surrey RH5 6HA, England.
- **Environmental Defense Fund:** 1616 P St., N.W., Washington, DC 20036; 1-800-CALL-EDF.
- **Farm Animal Rangers:** (FAR is the kids' group of Compassion

in World Farming) 20 Lavant St., Petersfield, Hampshire GU32 3EW, England.

- **Focus on Animals:** P.O. Box 150, Trumball, CT 06611.
- **Fox Cubs:** P.O. Box 1, Carlton, Nottingham NG4 25Y, England.
- **Friends of Animals:** P.O. Box 1244, Norwalk, CT 06856.
- **Friends of Animals Low-Cost Spay/Neuter Hotline:** 1-800-631-2212.
- **Friends of Washoe:** Central Washington University, Ellensburg, WA 98926.
- **The Fund for Animals:** 200 West 57th St., New York, NY 10019.
- **Greenpeace:** 1611 Connecticut Ave., N.W., Washington, DC 20016.
- **Greyhound Friends:** 167 Saddle Hill Rd., Hopkinton, MA 01748.
- **Greyhound Pets of America:** P.O. Box 3235, San Diego, CA 91773-2838.
- **Hooved Animal Humane Society:** P.O. Box 1099, Woodstock, IL 60098.
- **HOWL:** the PAWS Wildlife Center, Box 1037, Lynnwood, WA 98046.
- **Humane Society of the United States (HSUS):** 2100 L St., N.W., Washington, DC 20037.
- **Indiana Hooved Animal Humane Society:** P.O. Box 500, Morocco, IN 47963.
- **International Fund for Animal Welfare (IFAW):** Box 193, Yarmouth Port, MA 02675.
- **International Wildlife Rehabilitation Council (IWRC):** 4437 Central Place, Suite B4, Suisan, CA 94585.
- **The Kindness Club:** 65 Brunswick St., Fredericton, New Brunswick E3B 1G5, Canada.
- **Marin Humane Society:** 171 Bel Marin Keys Blvd., Novato, CA 94949.
- **Massachusetts Society for the Prevention of Cruelty to Animals (MSPCA):** 350 South Huntington Ave., Boston, MA 02130.
- **Minnesota Department of Natural Resources:** 500 Lafayette Rd., St. Paul, MN 55155.
- **National Association for Humane and Environmental Education (NAHEE):** 67 Salem Rd., East Haddam, CT 06423-0362.
- **National Humane Education Society (NHES):** 15-B Catoctin Circle S.E. #207, Leesburg, VA 22075.

- **National Society of Musicians for Animals:** P.O. Box 436, Redding Ridge, CT 06876.
- **National Wildlife Rehabilitation Association (NWRA):** 708 Riverside Ave. So., Sartrell, MN 56377.
- **New England Anti-Vivisection Society (NEAVS):** 333 Washington St., Suite 850, Boston, MA 02108-5100.
- **Peninsula Humane Society and Peninsula Humane Society Wildlife Center:** 12 Airport Blvd., San Mateo, CA 94401.
- **People for the Ethical Treatment of Animals (PETA):** P.O. Box 42516, Washington, DC 20015.
- **Performing Animal Welfare Society (PAWS):** P.O. Box 842, Galt, CA 95632.
- **Physicians Committee for Responsible Medicine (PCRM):** P.O. Box 6322, Washington, DC 20015.
- **Progressive Animal Welfare Society (PAWS):** P.O. Box 1037, Lynnwood, WA 98046.
- **Project Trees for Life:** 1103 Jefferson, Wichita, KS 67203.
- **Rainforest Action Network (RAN):** 301 Broadway, Suite A, San Francisco, CA 94133.
- **Rat Allies:** P.O. Box 3453, Portland, OR 97208.
- **Reptile Defense Fund:** 5025 Tulane Dr., Baton Rouge, LA 70808.
- **Retired Greyhounds as Pets:** P.O. Box 41307, St. Petersburg, FL 33743.
- **Rocky Mountain Humane Society:** P.O. Box 1250, Littleton, CO 80160.
- **San Francisco Society for the Prevention of Cruelty to Animals:** 2500 16th St., San Francisco, CA 94103.
- **School Campaign for Reaction Against Meat (SCREAM):** Parkdale, Dunham Road, Altrincham, Cheshire WA14 4QG, England.
- **Sea Shepherd Society:** P.O. Box 7000-S, Redondo Beach, CA 90277.
- **The Singing Rainbows:** c/o Sister's Choice, 1450 Sixth St., Berkeley, CA 94710.
- **Society for Animal Protective Legislation:** P.O. Box 3719, Washington, DC 20007.
- **Society for the Prevention of Cruelty to Animals of Monterey:** P.O. Box 3058, Monterey, CA 93940.
- **South Carolina Association for Marine Mammal Protection (SCAMMP):** P.O. Box 3233, Myrtle Beach, SC 29578-3233.

- **St. Louis Humane Society:** 1210 Macklind Rd., St. Louis, MO 63110.
- **Student Action Corps for Animals (SACA):** P.O. Box 15588, Washington, DC 20003–0588.
- **Suncoast Seabird Sanctuary:** 18328 Gulf Boulevard, Indian Shores, FL 33535.
- **Unexpected Wildlife Refuge:** P.O. Box 765, Newfield, NJ 08344.
- **United Activists for Animal Rights:** P.O. Box 2448, Riverside, CA 92516.
- **University of Minnesota Wildlife Rehabilitation Clinic:** St. Paul, MN 55108.
- **Vegetarian Resource Group:** P.O. Box 1463, Baltimore, MD 21203.
- **Vegetarian Society of the United Kingdom:** Parkdale, Dunham Road, Altrincham, Cheshire WA14 4QG, England.
- **Washington Humane Society (WHS):** 7319 Georgia Ave., N.W., Washington, DC 20012.
- **Wild Animal Rehabilitation Center:** 5800 North Lovers Lane Rd., Milwaukee, WI 53225.
- **Wildlife Center of Virginia:** Box 98, Weyers Cave, VA 24486.
- **Wildlife Rescue Association, B.C.:** 5216 Glencarin Dr., Burnaby, B.C. V5B 3C1 Canada.
- **Wildlife Rescue Inc.:** Box 15223, Austin, TX 78781-5223.
- **Willowbrook Wildlife Haven:** 525 S. Park Blvd., Glen Ellyn, IL 60137.
- **Zoo Check:** Cherry Tree Cottage, Coldharbour Lane, Dorking, Surrey RH5 6HA, England.

Note: There are many wonderful organizations that don't appear here. Contact PETA or your local animal shelter for one near you.

MAGAZINES AND NEWSLETTERS

- *Animal Aid Youth Group* **Newsletter:** 7 Castle St., Tonbridge, Kent TN9 1BH, England.
- *The Animals' Agenda:* P.O. Box 6809, Syracuse, NY 13217. 1-800-825-0061. The magazine will send a free issue to anyone who asks for a copy.

- *The Animals' Voice* **Magazine:** P.O. Box 1649, Martinez, CA 94533-9868; 1-800-82-VOICE.
- *The Beaver Defenders:* Unexpected Wildlife Refuge, P.O. Box 765, Newfield, NJ 08344.
- *Critters and Kids Chronicle:* Peninsula Humane Society, 12 Airport Blvd., San Mateo, CA 94401.
- *The Dolphin Log:* The Cousteau Society Membership Center, 930 West 21st St., Norfolk, VA 23517 ($10 per year).
- *Fox Cubs:* P.O. Box 1, Carlton, Nottingham NG4 25Y, England.
- *Greenscene:* Vegetarian Society, Parkdale, Dunham Road, Altrincham, Cheshire WA14 4QG, England.
- *Kind News Jr.* **(Grades 2–4),** *Kind News Sr.* **(Grades 5–6), and** *Kind Teacher:* National Association for Humane and Environmental Education (NAHEE), 67 Salem Rd., East Haddam, CT 06423. (Note: subscriptions, in packs of thirty-two for $20, available only to teachers, but anyone can receive one free issue with a self-addressed, stamped envelope.)
- *Otterwise:* P.O. Box 1374, Portland, ME 04104 ($4 per year).
- *OUT:* The Magazine for Farm Animal Rangers, Compassion in World Farming, 20 Lavant St., Petersfield, Hampshire GU32 3EW, England.
- *PETA Kids:* P.O. Box 42516, Washington, DC 20015 ($3 per year).
- *P–3: The Earth-Based Magazine for Kids:* P.O. Box 52, Montgomery, VT 05471 ($14 per year).
- *Trumpet*: Cherry Tree Cottage, Coldharbour Lane, Dorking, Surrey RH5 6HA, England.
- *Your Kindness Club Letter:* The Kindness Club, 65 Brunswick St., Fredericton, New Brunswick E3B 1G5, Canada ($2 per year).

BUSINESSES

- **Aesop Unlimited:** Dept. 304, P.O. Box 315, Cambridge, MA 02140.
- **Allen's Naturally:** P.O. Box 339, Dept. A, Farmington, MI 48332–0514.
- **Amberwood:** Rte. 1, Box 206, Milner, GA 30257.

- **Animal Town:** P.O. Box 2002, Santa Barbara, CA 93120.
- **Colour Quest:** 616 Third St., St. Charles, IL 60174.
- **Compassion Cosmetics:** P.O. Box 3534, Glendale, CA 91201.
- **Earth Care Paper Company:** 325 Beech Lane, Harbor Springs, MI 49740.
- **The Ecology House:** 1441 Pearl St., Boulder, CO 80302.
- **The Ecology House:** 49 Exchange St., Portland, ME 04101.
- **The Ecology House:** 341 S.W. Morrison, Portland, OR 97204.
- **Harbingers of a New Age:** 12100 Brighton St., Hayden Lake, ID 83835.
- **Heartland Products, Ltd.:** Box 218, Dakota City, IA 50529.
- **Interspecies Communication:** 273 Hidden Meadow Lane, Friday Harbor, WA 98250.
- **Lion and Lamb, Inc.:** 28-29 41st Ave., Suite 813, Long Island City, NY 11101.
- **Loma Linda Foods:** 1-800-932-5525.
- **Metro Stamp and Seal Company:** 9425 Georgia Avenue, Silver Spring, MD 20910.
- **National Dog Registry:** Box 116, Woodstock, NY 12498; 1-800-NDR-DOGS.
- **The Nature Company:** P.O. Box 2310, Berkeley, CA 94702; 1-800-227-1114.
- **Nike:** 1-800-344-NIKE.
- **Nobull Foods:** 6987 N. Oracle Rd., Suite 105, Tucson, AZ 85704; 1-800-828-7648.
- **Patagonia:** 1609 West Babcock St., P.O. Box 8900, Bozeman, MT 59715-2046; 1-800-336-9090.
- **PETA Merchandise:** P.O. Box 42400, Washington, DC 20015.
- **Seventh Generation:** Colchester, VT 05446-1672; 1-800-456-1177.
- **SMA Industries:** 3848 Del Amo #304, Torrence, CA 90503.
- **Spalding:** 1-800-642-5004.
- **Tattoo-A-Pet:** 1625 Emmons Ave., Suite 1H, Brooklyn, NY 11235; 1-800-828-8667.
- **Teaching Concepts, Inc.:** P.O. Box 150, Jericho, NY 11753.
- **Turtles, Inc.:** 111 Carpenter Ave., Sea Cliff, NY 11579.
- **Vegetarian Times:** P.O. Box 570, Oak Park, IL 60303.

ONE LAST THING YOU CAN DO TO SAVE THE ANIMALS

When you have finished this book, please consider passing it on to a friend or giving it to your local library. That way *many* others will learn how to join you in saving the animals! Thank you.